THE MYSTERY OF FORREST'S CAVE

A LT. KATE GAZZARA NOVEL

THE LT. KATE GAZZARA MURDER FILES
BOOK 21

BLAIR HOWARD

Disclaimer: The Mystery of Forrest's Cave is a work of fiction. No resemblance to actual persons or events is intended. Forrest's Cave is a figment of the author's imagination.

Product names, businesses, brands, and other trademarks referred to within this book are the property of the respective trademark holders and are used fictitiously. Unless otherwise specified, no association between the author and any trademark holder is expressed or implied. Nor does the use of such trademarks indicate an endorsement of the products, trademarks, or trademark holders unless so stated. Use of a term in this book should not be regarded as affecting the validity of any trademark, registered trademark, or service mark.

For Jo

1

Tuesday November 14, 2023

2:35PM

THE HYDRAULIC SAW'S whine echoed through Forrest's Cave, its diamond-tipped blade sending crystalline limestone dust dancing in the beams of the work lights. The mechanical growl bounced off the ancient walls that had known nothing but silence for millennia until tourism made its inevitable march underground. Crew chief Marcus Webb stood by, watching as his team carefully widened the passage, their movements practiced despite the confined space. The cave's naturally high humidity, mingled with sweat and pulverized stone, created a thick haze that clung to their safety gear and safety glasses and turned their reflective vests into ghostly shapes in the artificial light.

The expansion project had been underway for a little more than three weeks, transforming the historic cave system into something more... accommodating for modern-day visitors. Marcus had overseen similar renovations throughout the Southeast, but there was something about Forrest's Cave that made the hair on the back of his neck stand up. Maybe it was the way sound carried differently here, or how the shadows seemed to linger just a little longer than they should. He didn't know, but what he did know was that whatever it was, it bothered him.

"Two more inches should do it," Marcus called out, consulting the expansion plans spread across his makeshift workstation. The tourist path needed to accommodate modern accessibility standards. It would have been a simple enough job, had it not been for the cave's tendency to reveal its secrets at the most inconvenient times. He'd already discovered three new passages that weren't on any existing map, each requiring additional permits and expensive geological surveys before the work could continue.

He watched as apprentice Sara Hooper maneuvered her rotary hammer's carbide-tipped bit along the wall's edge some four hundred feet from the cave entrance where natural light still mingled with artificial illumination. The limestone was heavily weathered, marked by centuries of water erosion. Sara had been working in the caves for a little less than a year, but even she felt there was something about this section that felt different. The rock composition changed subtly here, displaying bands of darker material that didn't match the surrounding structure.

Her tool suddenly caught on something, the bit skittering across an unexpected void. The sound was wrong—hollow where it should have been solid, resonant where it should have been dead.

"Hold up," she said, killing the power. She leaned in closer, squinting through her safety glasses. Her light from her LED headlamp caught something pale against the darker stone. Something curved. Something wrong. Her mind tried to make sense of what she was seeing, to force it into familiar categories of geological formations, but failed.

"Marcus?" Her voice tremored. The crew chief looked up sharply. "I think you need to see this," she said.

The crew chief dropped what he was doing, grabbed a cloth wipe, wiped his brow, then his hands, then he dropped the cloth on his makeshift desk, grabbed a rolled up blueprint and quickly crossed the uneven ground to where she was standing, her face white as a sheet in the unnatural light of his headlamp.

"What?" he asked.

She pointed. He saw it, frowned, took a step forward, leaned in closer and he stared at it, the blueprint in his hand forgotten.

"Stop what you're doing!" he shouted. And the work site instantly transformed into a silent, frozen tableau. The skeletal hand, covered in glistening limestone secretion, protruded from the newly exposed crevice as if it was offering a macabre greeting, its phalanges partially encased in calcite deposits.

"Everyone… out of here, now!" Marcus yelled. "Put down your tools and go. Touch nothing." He turned to Sara. "You, too," he said, then he ran to the cave entrance and called 911, the dust slowly settling behind him in the harsh light of the work lamps.

The next hour passed in a blur of police radio calls and camera flashes. The cave, usually so peaceful at that time of day, buzzed with a nervous energy as local law enforcement established a perimeter and began documenting the scene. Their boots, unused to the cave's treacherous footing, scraped and slipped on the limestone floor.

Dr. Amelia Croft, her long, auburn hair pulled back in a practical braid under her safety helmet, arrived just as the first news vans were parking outside the cave entrance. She hurried to the police tape, acknowledged the detective's presence with a brief nod, held up her credentials and ducked under the tape before the reporters could get to her. Her focus was and had to be entirely on the scene before her. Twenty years of studying cave systems had taught her that first impressions were crucial—the moment when the cave revealed its stories to those who knew how to read them.

"No one's touched anything?" she asked, unslinging her equipment pack. The cave's cool air raised goosebumps on her arms despite her long-sleeved thermal shirt.

"Site's exactly as we found it, ma'am," Marcus confirmed, grateful for a professional's presence. "Four hundred feet in, they were widening the tourist path when—"

"Show me the original expansion plans," Amelia interrupted him, already pulling out her pocket transit compass. She studied the blueprints briefly, her eyes narrowing at several notations from the 1970s. "And the blueprints from the latest survey?" She asked.

He slid them to her across the makeshift desk. She stared at one, then the other, then she repeated the process several times. Then she shook her head, still looking down at the latest blueprint. "These old survey marks suggest there were previous modifications that weren't fully documented," she said, thoughtfully, then looked at Marcus.

He shrugged. "It's what the powers that be provided. How accurate they are is anyone's guess."

"Guess? That's not what we do, Chief," she said, dryly. "Are there any later blueprints?"

"No, ma'am," he replied, uncomfortably.

She nodded. He returned the nod and said, "if you'll follow me…"

She followed him into the cave and began her systematic assessment, falling into the familiar rhythm of scientific observation.

Her headlamp illuminated the breakdown zone in harsh detail. The cave's history was written on its walls—the chaotic pattern of ancient ceiling collapse, the slow accretion of flowstone, and now, this newer chapter. She used her laser meter to take precise measurements, speaking quietly into her digital recorder as she did so. The familiar routine helped her maintain professional distance, not just from the crew chief, but also from the gruesome discovery.

"Subject location is approximately one-point-two meters above current floor level, oriented horizontally, based on visible remains. Phalanges show significant speleothem formation, with calcite deposits consistent with decades of exposure." She peered closer, careful not to disturb anything. "There are tool marks visible in the surrounding matrix... The distinctive patterning suggests mechanical expansion, likely from the 1973 development project."

The detective, a heavyset man whose name tag read "Harrison," shifted impatiently behind her. From his shallow breathing and nervous adjustments to his collar, it was obvious he was uncomfortable in the underground environment.

"Can you give me a timeframe?" he asked.

Amelia's light played across the exposed bone, highlighting the delicate stalagmite formations that had grown between the fingers. The cave had been slowly claiming these remains, transforming human tragedy into mineral beauty, for a long time.

"Based on the flowstone development and calcification patterns," she said thoughtfully. "I'd say... mid-sixties, early seventies. See these mineral deposits?" She pointed with a laser pointer, tracing the delicate structures. "They take decades to form under these conditions." She squinted and looked up into the dark roof, her headlamp casting stark shadows as it played across the rocky formations.

Harrison nodded, then turned away and made a beeline for the cave entrance and the fresh air beyond.

Amelia smiled as she continued her examination of the scene, documenting every detail. The surrounding breakdown zone told a complex story of part natural collapse, part human modification. The body's position suggested it had been deliberately placed rather than accidentally trapped. *Someone knew enough*

9

about cave systems to find this spot, far enough from the then tourist areas to remain undiscovered for decades, she thought.

Marcus stood back and watched as she worked. The cave's atmosphere had changed since the discovery. The usual peaceful silence had given way to whispered conversations and the click of camera shutters. Even the air felt different, as if the cave itself was awakening to the disturbance of its long-held secrets. He shuddered at the thought.

As she adjusted her position to examine the crevice's depth, the beam of her headlamp caught something else. About eighteen inches beyond the hand, something metallic glittered, reflecting the light. The reflection was too regular, too smooth to be a natural cave formation. *Whatever it is,* she thought, *it's looks to me as if it was placed there deliberately, likely at the same time as the body.*

"There's something else in here," she said, holding her recorder close to her mouth and angling her light for a better view. "The object appears to be curved, possibly circular. A bracelet, perhaps. The position suggests it might have deliberately placed, though decades of mineral deposits make it difficult to be certain."

Detective Harrison, now returned, leaned in over her shoulder. His foot slipped, sending a cascade of loose pebbles skittering across the cave floor. "Can you reach it?" he asked.

Amelia shook her head, already cataloging the equipment she'd need for a proper excavation. "Not without compromising the scene. But whatever it is, it's not geological in origin." She sat back on her heels, her mind already racing through possibilities. This wasn't just a simple recovery operation anymore. The cave's geology, the time frame, the deliberate placement; it all pointed to something much more complex. "We're going to need a full forensic team in here. And I'll need to map the entire surrounding cave system. Something tells me this is just the beginning. I'll make the call." And she did.

The cave's cool air currents whispered around them, and

Amelia shivered involuntarily as she felt the familiar tingle of scientific curiosity mixing with something darker; the understanding that she was now part of this cave's ongoing story. Above them, barely visible in the artificial light, water droplets continued their never-ending reshaping of the stone, indifferent to the human drama unfolding below.

Marcus returned to the cave entrance and gathered his crew, their faces pale in the light of the discovery.

"You can all go home," he said, loudly. "The work will be delayed indefinitely, but stay in touch. I know it's tough, but it is what it is."

And they went, muttering among themselves.

He returned to the cave, concerned that he'd had to lay off the crew, but that seemed insignificant compared to what they'd uncovered.

Amelia continued dictating preliminary notes for her report, conscious of the feeling she'd be spending a lot more time in Forrest's Cave than she'd initially planned. The mystery was here, preserved in stone and mineral deposits, waiting for someone with the right skills to uncover it, and she was determined to be the one to unravel it.

She finished her report, turned off the recorder, slipped it into her pocket and stared at the bones. They remained as they'd found them. The calcified fingers seemed to be pointing deeper into the darkness, as if gesturing toward secrets yet to be revealed.

She took a deep breath, stared into the darkness, shivered, and then turned again to the bones and started work.

Mike Willis and his forensics team arrived with their specialized equipment at a little after nine the following morning.

2

Wednesday Morning

Kate

    8:30am

IT WAS one of those wild and windy mornings in November and I'd barely had time to park my car and push through the rear door when my phone rang. I looked at the screen. It was the chief so, as I was already in the corridor and outside his office door, I knocked, opened the door and stepped into his outer office to be greeted by his secretary Cindy with a bright and cheery Good Morning, though I wasn't feeling either bright or cheery.

She smiled up at me and said, "Good timing, Captain. He's waiting for you."

I heaved a sigh, nodded, and stepped up to his door, tapped twice, opened it, stuck my head inside and said, "You called. I'm here."

But, as usual, he didn't see the humor in it, saying instead,

"Come on in, Kate. Take a seat. Hi, Samson," he added, giving my dog a rare smile.

"You giving them away, then?" I asked cheerily.

He gave me a wry look and said, "Sit down, Captain." And I did.

I sat down in one of the two over-stuffed, wing-back chairs in front of his desk, folded my hands demurely in my lap, cocked my head to one side and smiled at him.

"What is wrong with you today?" he growled.

"Not a thing, Chief," I replied. "I'm good. What's the haps?"

"We have a situation," he replied, then paused and regarded me, as if trying to find the right words.

"Don't we always?" I asked.

He ignored the question. "Yesterday afternoon, I had a call from Chief Lawrence," he began, then paused again.

"Lookout Mountain?" I asked.

He nodded, then said, "Did you know they're working underground again in Forrest's Cave?"

"I heard something about it," I replied, "but just in passing. Why?" I frowned. "How does that affect us?"

"Apparently, they found something... A hand, or what's left of it. It's old, so the expert said. Anyway, Lookout Mountain is a small department and Lawrence asked me to help out. It's not the first time." He paused, locked eyes with me, and continued. "Anyway, I told him we would, and I sent Willis and his crew up there this morning." He looked at his watch, then continued. "He should be arriving there anytime now. But now Lawrence tells me they need an experienced detective. That's where you come in, Kate. I want you to assign someone to take a look at it. It's the least we can do. I'm thinking that renegade of yours, Jack North. His family has a history with those caves. His grandfather was the lead detective in a series of disappearances back in the sixties and seventies. Makes young North the ideal candidate, don't you think?"

Chapter 2

In truth, I didn't know what to think, so I shrugged, made a face, then said, "And when, exactly, does this need to happen?"

"Right away. They've had to shut down their operation; very expensive. So go have a word with him. Have him go on up there and report back to you with his findings. We'll figure it out from there. That's all, Captain."

I had been summarily dismissed.

So I stood and waited for him to say something more, but he didn't. He was already flipping through the screens on his computer, so I turned and Samson led me to the door and I opened it.

"Kate!"

I turned to look at him.

"Keep an eye on him."

I nodded. "You bet, Chief."

AND SO IT BEGAN, a case that... Well, the story of the case of Forrest's Cave is a strange and complex one, and while I had overall jurisdiction, it's really Jack's story, so I'll tell it to you as it unfolded as best I can.

Detective Jack North is... a seasoned, though somewhat undisciplined investigator and computer wiz in his mid thirties. He was assigned to my team almost two years ago as a last resort. I was his last stop before dismissal from the force. Fortunately for him and for me, he's since managed to keep his nose clean. Well, relatively clean. He's a good detective, well-liked by me and the rest of the team, and because of his computer skills, extremely useful. But he can be a handful and has a nasty habit of going off on his own without telling anyone what he's up to; a trait that's gotten him into trouble with Internal Affairs many times over the years. His problem is, he's dedicated, pig-headed and opinionated. I've always kept him on a short leash, but this... I already knew it had disaster written all over it.

So, I left the chief and went to my office, tapping Jack on the shoulder and gestured for him to follow me along the way. He has a desk in the situation room, though he spends more time in the computer lab than he does there.

"Sit down, Jack," I said as I took my seat behind my desk and Samson flopped down in his bed under the window.

Jack frowned at me as he sat down, then said, "Am I in trouble, boss?"

"No, not at all," I replied. "I have a job for you, but first, I need you to tell me about your grandfather and his connection to the caves on Lookout Mountain."

Jack looked at me, still frowning. He was wearing his trademark worn leather jacket over a rumpled dress shirt, open at the neck, his badge and department-issued Glock 22 holstered at his hip.

He's thirty-six, divorced with no children, a quite nice-looking man of medium build. At five-feet-ten and maybe a hundred and seventy pounds, he's a little shorter than me, but then most people are. Clean shaven, hair cut short over his ears, and a somewhat disarming, naturally outgoing personality. He's also not one to suffer fools lightly, something else that always bothered me when sending him out on his own. Still, the chief thought he was the man for the job, and who was I to argue with that? As I've already mentioned, Jack had long been a headache for Internal Affairs. His unorthodox approach included maintaining a personal database of cold cases on a custom-built rig in his apartment, something that skirts department IT protocols but has cracked more than one forgotten case.

"My grandfather?" he asked. "What's he got to do with anything?"

"According to the chief," I replied, "he was the lead detective for a case involving a series of disappearances on Lookout Mountain."

"Ye-s," he said, slowly nodding his head.

"So," I said. "Come on, Jack. Give. What d'you know about it?"

"Me? Nothing. The old man's been dead eight years this Christmas. I didn't know him that well. He was very sick toward the end. He never talked about it. Not to me, anyway."

I sighed and shook my head.

"What?" he asked.

"There's been a find in Forrest's Cave. The chief wants you to take it on."

"Really?" he said, brightening up. "What have they found? And why us?"

"The Lookout Mountain PD is shorthanded, and they don't have the necessary resources to carry out an in-depth investigation..." I paused, then said, "Chief Lawrence asked for mutual aid, so we're it. Mike Willis and his crew are already on site. You'll be coordinating with a Detective Harrison and a geologist, Doctor Amelia Croft. You're to go right away. The site work has been shut down for the duration. Questions?"

"Yeah, dozens, but none I want to air right now," he replied. "I'm on my own, then?"

I pursed my lips and nodded. "I don't know how long you'll be up there, but I need you to report in daily and run any needs you might have through me. Understood?"

He nodded and started to rise.

"One more thing, Jack," I said, and he sat back down again. "No nonsense up there. Got it? You're a hothead and I don't want this to be your last hoorah. Take it easy, do your job, and don't make waves."

He nodded, grinned at me, and said, "Me, a hothead? Are you serious, boss?"

"I am. Keep your nose clean. I'm relying on you."

"You got it, Captain." And with that, he stood up and quickly left the room. He also left me wondering what the hell I'd gotten myself into because, no matter what antics Jack might get up to, the buck stopped with me.

3

Wednesday Morning

JACK

10am

In the cave

JACK ARRIVED on site at a little after ten that morning to find Detective Harrison waiting for him in the site office. Dr. Croft hadn't yet arrived. She was still at her office at UTC.

Jack and Harrison exchanged the usual greetings—though Harrison seemed a little reserved, perhaps even perturbed as he introduced Jack to the site manager Marcus Webb.

"So, what exactly have you found?" Jack asked, neither one of them in particular.

Webb looked at Harrison, then at Jack and said, "Best thing to do is go take a look, shall we…? I can't introduce you to Amelia, the lady in charge. She's not here."

"She's in charge?" Jack frowned. "How can she be in charge? When will she be back?"

"Hard to say," Webb said as he handed him a hard hat. "This afternoon, tomorrow. Who knows with these academic types?"

Jack nodded and together, the three men walked to the cave entrance, where they found Mike Willis talking to two members of his team. At the sound of their approach, Willis turned, saw Jack, smiled and held out his hand.

"Jack," he said. "What are you doing here?"

"Hey, Mike. I'm wondering about that myself. Kate assigned the case to me." He replied, noting Harrison's deepening frown. "What do we have here?"

"We have what appears to be a complete skeleton," Willis replied. "Fortunately, it's been almost completely excavated by the geologist—a most meticulous young lady, if I may say so. I'll walk with you. The entrance to the cavern is partially collapsed, and the passage is narrow, so we have to be careful."

"A native American burial?" Jack asked, noting Harrison's skeptical expression.

Willis shook his head. "Nope. It's not that old. Fifty or sixty years, according to Amelia." He pointed. "There. See?"

The scene—basically a small crevice some six feet by six by six in the cave wall—had been taped off and was well lit by three Nomad portable spotlights.

"Mike, you and me," Jack said. "Mr. Webb, you and Detective Harrison stay here while we take a look."

"But—" Harrison began but stopped when he saw the look on Jack's face. Then, he took a breath and said, "This is my case, Detective. I was first on the—"

"Look," Jack said, interrupting him. "If you have a problem, take it up with your chief. He reached out to us and I was assigned the case. Now, if you don't mind, I'd like to look at the body."

Harrison set his jaw, then nodded.

Jack returned his nod, then lifted the tape and ducked under, followed by Mike Willis.

The body was much as Willis had described it: a complete skeleton laid out straight, almost completely excavated, with only the feet still to be uncovered.

Hmm... Looks posed, he thought, *but how, and why?* "What's that, Mike?" he asked, pointing to the metallic object.

"We think it might be a bracelet," Willis replied. "I think it's probably silver. One of those medical alert bracelets, perhaps."

Jack nodded thoughtfully. "Makes sense," he said.

He looked around, taking note of his surroundings, then said,

"What are you thinking, Jack?" Willis asked.

"Not sure, but I'm wondering how this person got here and was he or she still alive or did someone dump the body here, and if so, when and how?"

"There's no good answer to any of that," Willis replied. "What I can tell you is that we're some four-hundred feet into the cave system, in a chamber that wasn't excavated until 1998 and, in the sixties and seventies, would probably have required professional caving gear to access. Amelia thinks the remains have been here at least fifty, perhaps as many as sixty years, thus establishing the time of death to be somewhere in the mid to late seventies."

Geez, this is not what I signed up for, Jack thought. *I know nothing about this kind of... Ah, what the hell?*

"Okay, here's the plan," he said. "We call in Doc Sheddon and see what he has to—"

"You're going to call in the medical examiner?" Harrison interrupted him. "Why would you do that? It's obviously an accidental death."

"You're wrong, Detective," Jack said. "This isn't some random body dump. The positioning of the body is deliberate. I'm no caver, but even I can see there's no equipment, no evidence that this person was equipped for caving and, back in the seventies, I'm pretty damn sure this cavern and its approaches would have been rated difficult. No, someone knew these caves. Knew them well enough to carry or drag the body in here in complete darkness. What we have here is a homicide. I'm calling Doc Sheddon."

Despite Harrison's protests about jurisdiction and procedure, Jack went back to the cave entrance and made the call.

He looked at his watch. *Geez,* he thought, *it's after eleven-thirty. He'll be going to lunch soon.*

He searched through his contacts, found the one he was looking for, and hit send.

"Doctor Sheddon's office. How can I help you?"

"Hi. Good morning. This is Detective North. I'd like to speak to Doc, please."

"I'll see if he can take your call. May I say what it's about?"

"No. Just tell him it's important."

"Hold, please."

And then he waited.

"Jack North," Doc said. "This is a surprise. What can I do for you, son?"

"I'm at Forrest's Cave, up on the mountain, and I have a body... well, the remains of a body. Can you come, like now?"

"That's pushing it a little," he replied. "I'm in the middle of writing... Remains, you say?"

"A full skeleton, by the look of it," Jack replied.

"Condition?"

"It's complete, if that's what you mean?"

"No, that's not what I meant, but never mind." Doc paused for a moment, then continued, "Forrest's Cave, you say? Well, give me forty-five minutes."

"You'll need a hard hat," Jack said. "Do you have one? If not, I'll have the site manager provide one for you."

"I have one, Jack, but thank you."

Dr. Richard Sheddon, the Hamilton County Chief Medical Examiner, arrived thirty minutes later.

A small man in his late fifties, a little over five-eight, over-weight, bald, with a round face and a seemingly permanent jolly expression, Doc was a popular addition to any investigative team.

"That was quick," Jack said, as Sheddon exited the big black SUV.

"Better early than late, Jack," he replied as he went around the back of the big vehicle and retrieved his big black bag. "Well, lead on. Where is it?"

Jack led him to the scene where Harrison was talking to Mike Willis. They both shook hands with Doc, though Harrison's mood obviously hadn't changed. Then, Jack stood by while Doc made his initial examination.

After maybe five minutes, Doc stood up and motioned for Jack to come closer.

"My first thought was that the perimortem fractures are inconsistent with a climbing accident. There are also multiple defensive wounds on the ulna and radius, see?" He pointed.

Jack leaned in closer, nodded, then said, "Knife wounds?"

"Possibly," Doc replied. "If so, it would've had to have been a big one, a large hunting knife, perhaps. There's also blunt force trauma to the occipital bone." He gently lifted the skull. "See?"

Again, Jack nodded, but then shook his head and said, "I wonder who it is and how they got here?"

"The teeth look good," Doc replied, "so there may be dental records and maybe even some DNA. It shouldn't be too difficult to find out."

"A familial match?" Jack asked.

"At the very least," Doc replied. "I need to transfer the remains to my lab, but we need to release the feet first." He turned and looked at Willis and said, "Mike?"

"Yes, of course," Willis replied. "Can you give me say... an hour?"

Doc looked at his watch, then nodded and was about to speak when Harrison beat him to it.

"Now wait just a minute," Harrison snapped. "You can't just—"

"And just what would you do, Detective?" Jack said, cutting him off.

"It's not your—"

"Your chief made it my jurisdiction when he invoked mutual aid and called us in. Now, as I see it, you can either cooperate or get the hell out of the way. Which is it to be?"

Harrison gave Jack a look that would have turned a lesser man to jelly, but he hesitated, then nodded and backed down.

"You were about to say something, Doc?" Jack asked.

"Walk with me, Jack," he replied. "I find the caves a little claustrophobic."

And together, they slowly made their way back to the cave entrance.

"There's no doubt that what we have here is a homicide, Jack," Doc said as they walked out into the watery sunshine. "And at least fifty years cold. It's going to be quite a challenge. You think you're up for it?"

"Did you know that my dear old granddad, Lieutenant Charlie North, was the lead detective on a case here on the mountain that involved several disappearances back in the sixties and seventies? I have a feeling our friend down there might be one of them. The case was never solved. So it's funny, don't you think, that it should fall to me to solve it? So yes, I'm up for it."

"I didn't know that, about your grandfather. Is he still with us?"

"Unfortunately, no. He passed eight years ago."

"Pity," Doc said. "I'm sure he would have been a veritable mine of information. I have a folding stretcher in the back," he nodded toward his SUV. "I'll need a hand to transfer the remains, please."

"Of course," Jack replied, and then helped Doc get the stretcher out of the car and into the cave. When they arrived back at the scene, Mike Willis was still on his knees, carefully removing the remains of the secretion from the victim's feet.

Twenty minutes later, the bones had been laid on the stretcher and were on their way to the surface.

Doc drove away some ten minutes later, leaving Jack, Harrison and Willis staring after him.

After a few moments of thought, Jack turned to Webb, who'd rejoined them and said, "Any chance I could get a copy of your survey map?"

"Sure, I have several copies. Can I ask why?"

"Well, for one, I'd like to know what I'm dealing with; and for two, I want to see how it compares with those they were using back in the day."

Webb nodded and said, "Let's go to my office."

———

It was a little after five that afternoon, after making sure that Doc and his team had everything they needed, and that Harrison wasn't too bent out of shape by the events of the day, when Jack quit for the day.

He stopped in at the PD intending to bring Kate up to date with what was happening, but she'd already left, so he stopped in at Bud's for a quick drink, then at Domino's for a pizza—mushroom and pepperoni—and then he went home to his apartment.

He dumped the pizza and the roll of maps on the kitchen table, went to the fridge, took out a bottle of Coor's Lite, opened it and sat down at the table.

He took a drink of beer, swallowed noisily, then sat there staring thoughtfully at the roll of maps.

He grabbed a slice of pizza from the box, took a bite, chewed, swallowed, set the rest of the slice down on the bare tabletop, picked up his phone and called his mother.

"Jack," she said. "How nice. How are you? When are we going to see you?"

"Um, I'm fine. Thanks. I might drop by over the weekend, but it depends. I have a new case… which is why I called you. Where did you put Grandad Charlie's papers?"

"What papers are you talking about? We threw most of that stuff away when he passed—"

"His work papers, Mom," he interrupted her. "He had a file cabinet full of old case files and some boxes."

"Oh that," she replied. "Your dad hauled all of that old stuff away—"

"Oh geez. Are you serious? Can I talk to him?"

"Yes, of course. Let me hand him the phone."

Jack waited, listening to his mother talking in muffled tones to his father but not understanding a word.

"Jack," his father said a moment later. "You want Charlie's files? They're in a storage locker on Heath. You'll need to come and get the key."

"Thanks, Dad," Jack replied. "I'll be there in an hour, if that's okay?"

"You want me to go with you?" his father asked.

"No, but thanks. I'm not sure what I'm looking for, so it might take me a while. I'll just drop by and get the key."

Thirty minutes later, after a quick shower, a change of clothes and a slice of cold pizza, he headed out the door to his parent's home in North Chattanooga where, good as his word, his father had the key to the storage locker waiting for him.

"You sure you don't want me to come with you?" he asked as he handed it to him.

"Nope, I got it," he replied. "Tell mom hello for me and that I'll try to come by this weekend. Thanks, Dad."

Jacob North nodded and said, "The gate code is zero, two, seven, zero."

Another thirty minutes later, he was parked outside the storage locker, key and flashlight in hand. He opened the lock, raised the door and stepped inside.

He quickly found what he was looking for: two old, steel four-drawer file cabinets and a long steel box that had once held a dozen M-16 rifles.

He knelt down beside the box and opened it. Inside were, among other things, three cardboard cylinders with metal press-in caps. He smiled to himself. Took one from the box and read the handwritten label, Mine Operations – Lookout Mountain – 1896. The second cylinder had a similar label, but was dated 1877. He nodded, took out the third cylinder, set all three aside, and closed the box. Then he stood up and went to the cabinets and looked at the drawer labels, smiling to himself; his grandfather was nothing if not meticulous.

He found what he was looking for, pulled open the drawer, and, staring at the contents, he shook his head. The drawer was stuffed full of files, all related to what Charlie had called 'Missing!'

There were twenty-eight of them, each labeled by name, date and gender. The first was dated April 15, 1974, the last one September 10, 1998.

Geez, what the hell? he thought. *It'll take me a week just to read through these. Case notes... Where are his case notes?*

It took a while, but he eventually found them, two, three-inch ring binders stuffed full of papers and three manila concertina files full of photographs.

"Geez," he muttered. "What the hell was the old man into? Damn, I wish I could talk to him. Humm. I wonder."

He took out his phone and called Kate.

"Jack," she said. "It's almost nine-thirty. What d'you want? Can't it wait until morning?"

"Well… yeah, I suppose, but—"

"Good, I'll see you at the office bright and early, eight o'clock sharp." And she hung up.

Later that evening, having unloaded three banker's boxes full of files and the three cardboard cylinders into his apartment, Jack, seated himself in front of a bank of three computer monitors displaying census data and digitized newspaper archives, and, using a propriety, custom-built pattern-recognition algorithm running on hardware that would make the police department IT team, not to mention IA, apoplectic, he was able to flag the series of disappearances in Chattanooga and the tri-state area beginning in 1972 through 1998, but there were more than twenty-eight. By the time he called it quits, the number was sixty-one, dating from 1963 through 2008.

He stared at the list in awe. *What the hell have I gotten myself into?* He wondered.

4

Thursday Morning

JACK, much to my surprise, arrived on time that Thursday morning. He was waiting for me outside my office door when I arrived at eight, which wasn't exactly a first, but it was a rarity.

"Bright and early, is it?" I said, as I unlocked the door. I opened it and he followed Samson and me inside.

I set my coffee down on the desk and turned Sammy loose, then I sat down, took a sip of my coffee, and stared at him.

"Well," I said, "are you just going to stand there or are you going to sit down and tell me what the hell is going on?"

He sat down. Samson sat down beside him and looked up at him.

"It's about this case—" he began, fondling Sammy's ears.

"What case?" I asked. "It's not a case. I just asked you to take a look at what they found—"

"Oh, but you're wrong, boss," he said, interrupting me, leaning forward. "It's a case alright. You have no idea... Look, you know my grandfather, Lieutenant Charlie North, worked a number of missing person cases from '74 to '87—he took early retirement in '87, you know that, right?"

I nodded slowly, skeptically, and he continued.

"Well, he thought they were connected to the copper mining companies that were operating on Lookout Mountain at the time," he continued excitedly. "He wasn't able to prove it, of course, and the cases were never solved, and none of the missing people were ever found. But see, I think the body in the cave is one of the missing people. I mean, just take a look at these. They're just a sample. Seven missing people." He dumped a stack of files on my desk and continued, "1975, three women, ages nineteen to twenty-five, all last seen near mining company property. 1977, a mining company whistleblower and his wife. 1979, two more young women and a mine safety inspector. And there are more. Another twenty-one files, plus thirty-three more I found online, dating from 1963 through 2008. They all fit the pattern."

He paused for a moment, and I could tell there was more he wanted to say, so I waited.

"I also found his notes. There are stories about mining company men who 'took care of problems.' He made quotes with his finger around the words, took care of problems.

"Come and look at them," he said, standing up and grabbing the files. Then he turned around and spread them out on the table.

I remained seated, staring at him, so he continued, "I need copies of all the missing person files for the period, including..." And he ticked them off on his fingers.

· Missing persons' reports 1970-2023
· Mining company employee records
· Property maps and deed transfers

·   Unsealed grand jury testimony related to mining safety violations

·   Local newspaper archives, particularly focusing on the mining section

I slowly shook my head. "You've got to be kidding," I said. "One, it's going to raise a lot of hackles. Two, you want to expand a single body whose identity is still unknown into a full-blown murder investigation, and we don't even know if it's connected to your grandfather's case. Three, we don't have the budget. Four, the chief won't go for it, Jack."

"So why did you send me out there, then, if you don't want it investigated? Doc's already confirmed the death as a homicide. There's a damn great hole in the back of its head. And that detective the Mountain assigned to it is an idiot. He's already written it off as accidental. But there are defensive wounds on the—"

"All right, all right, Jack." I said, cutting him off. "Take it easy. If you can identify the remains as those of one of your missing sixty-one, well, we'll see about expansion. In the meantime, I want you investigating the remains in the cave; that's all; that's our mandate. And you report to me here daily. Understand?"

He grinned at me and nodded.

"I'm expecting Doctor Amelia Croft at nine," I said. "I want you to stay and meet her. You'll be working with her."

"What?" he asked, skeptically. "You want me to work with a civilian?"

"I do," I replied. "She's a geologist and an experienced caver, both of which you're not."

He blew out a breath, then glared at me and said, "Well… If you say so, I guess."

"I do say so." I replied, and would have said more, but there was a knock on the door and Cooper stuck his head inside and said , "There's a Doctor Amelia Croft here to see you. She says she has an appointment. You want me to show her in?"

I nodded. Cooper left. I looked at Jack and said, "You behave yourself. You hear?"

Amelia Croft was an attractive young woman of average height—about five-eight—and, so I noted, professionally dressed in a dark gray pant suit over a white blouse. Her auburn hair was tied back in a ponytail and her hazel eyes sparkled under the fluorescent lighting.

"Doctor Croft," I said, standing up and stepping around my desk, my hand extended in greeting. "It's nice to meet you. This is Detective Jack North. He's leading the investigation into the remains you found. Please, take a seat."

Jack offered her his hand. She smiled at him, nodded and shook his hand, and then took the seat in front of my desk. Jack pulled a chair from the table and sat down next to her.

"I assume I'm here because you'd like me to assist Detective North," she said.

I glanced at Jack and could see from his expression that he was skeptical.

I nodded. "Jack's an experienced investigator, as are you, so I understand. So yes, it would make sense for you to work together. Would that be a problem, Doctor?"

"Not at all… so long as he doesn't get in my way."

That wasn't what I wanted to hear.

"Then I'm sure the two of you will get along just fine, right, Jack?"

"As am I," she said. "I do wish, however, that he'd waited until I was present before he removed the remains. There's no telling how much damage might have been caused to crucial evidence."

Jack opened his mouth to speak, but before he could, I stepped in and said, "Jack didn't remove it. He simply ordered it removed to preserve the evidence. An experienced forensic supervisor and the chief medical examiner carried out the actual removal. If you wish to examine the remains, you can do so at the forensic center three blocks west of here."

"Yes, I'd like to do that," she replied. "In the meantime—"

"Doctor Croft," Jack said, cutting her off. "We think the remains are connected to a series of missing persons cases dating back into the early 1970s. Perhaps you'd like to take a look." And he directed her attention to the files on the table.

She looked at him, her eyes narrowed.

This is going to be a partnership made in hell, I thought as she stood up and turned to the table.

She stood for a moment, then reached out a finger flipped one of the files open and looked at the photo of a young girl. She pursed her lips, flipped open a second file, then a third, and then she then flipped open the file containing the photos taken of the remains in the cave and stared at them with barely concealed disapproval, her finger tracing the documented collection points with growing concern.

"These samples should have been bagged separately," she said, tapping a photograph showing mineral deposits. "Cross-contamination could compromise the chronological markers. When dealing with speleothems, even microscopic disturbances can—"

"With all due respect, Doctor," Jack interrupted, leaning forward, "what we have here is a homicide. The priority was to secure any evidence of foul play, not preserving your cave formations."

Amelia's jaw tightened. "Those 'cave formations' could tell us exactly when your victim was placed there. The calcite deposits in that chamber have distinct growth patterns. By analyzing the mineral layers that have accumulated over any disrupted areas, we can establish a fairly precise timeline."

Jack paused, his interest piqued despite his skepticism. Thirteen years on the force had taught him to trust his gut, but he couldn't deny the value of hard science. "How precise?"

"In optimal conditions? Within a few months, either way." She pulled her laptop out of her shoulder bag.

"This is a 3D scan of a cave system; it's not Forrest's Cave, of course. That's something I'll need to do. But see these flowstone curtains? They're essentially geological timekeepers. Any disturbance in the natural order of things leaves microscopic traces we can date."

Jack nodded slowly, reaching for his case notes. "So we could corroborate witness statements from 1968, then? There were three reports of suspicious activity around the cave entrance that summer, but the timestamps never quite lined up."

"Show me," Amelia said.

Inwardly, I had to smile. Jack was never the easiest person to get along with, much less work with, and I had no doubt that these were two of a kind. So I smiled as I watched her professional detachment softening slightly as Jack walked her through his investigation timeline. And I had no doubt that his understanding of human nature complemented her technical expertise. Where she saw geological evidence, he saw human patterns and possible motives.

"It seems you two have things to discuss," I said, rising to my feet. "So I'm going to leave you to it. I'll be back in an hour." And I left the room and went to see the chief.

Johnston was in one of his moods, so the visit was a short one. I filled him in on Jack's progress so far, and that he and Dr. Croft were in my office getting to know one another, then I went to the break room, poured myself a cup of really dreadful coffee, and then made my rounds of the rest of my team. By the time I was done, it was almost eleven thirty, so I went back to my office, where I found them wrapping it up.

Between them, they seemed to have agreed on a hybrid approach to the case that married forensic geology with traditional detective work. It was obvious to me, though, that neither fully trusted the other's methods, but both recognized the potential of their unlikely partnership. Amelia would re-analyze the cave samples while Jack would visit the old witnesses; those that were still alive.

As they packed up, I saw Jack glance at Amelia's meticulous notes and compare them to his own disorganized scratchings.

He looked at her, then at me and said, grudgingly, "This might actually work, I guess."

"It might," Croft agreed, closing her laptop. "If you can avoid contaminating any more of my crime scene."

"Your crime scene?" Jack arched an eyebrow.

"Our crime scene," she corrected, with just the hint of a smile. "For now."

I smiled to myself. It was as I thought, a partnership made in hell!

Thursday Afternoon

JACK & AMELIA

1pm

THE FLUORESCENT LIGHTS hummed overhead as Amelia stared at yet another stack of yellowing case files Jack dumped on the metal table in the police archives basement; the morgue, as it was popularly known to the detectives who haunted it. Twenty-eight cardboard banker's boxes; an untold number of yellowing folders fanned out across the table. Each box containing a life interrupted - eighteen women and nine men who simply vanished from the streets of Chattanooga during the 1970s and early 80s.

Amelia noticed the pattern immediately. "They're all young working-class victims, mostly from the Highland Park, East Lake, and Ridgedale areas. It looks to me as if their stories were buried as quickly as they disappeared." She shook her head and grimaced at the sheer immensity of the task before them.

"Is this all of them?" she asked.

"Not quite," Jack replied as he reached up and pulled down the Rebecca Carter file from 1974 frowning at the timestamp. "This was one of the first," he said. "She was a hooker... Sorry, I mean prostitute. Six man-hours," he muttered, more to himself than to Amelia. "That's all the time they spent investigating this one, a case with clear evidence of a struggle before she disappeared." He shook his head and heaved a sigh. "The other files," he nodded at the overloaded table, "they all tell a similar story. Two or three days of perfunctory investigation, then nothing. They went cold and ended up down here. Unless," he noted, "you were from the right family. I mean, the Van Horn girl's disappearance was front-page news for weeks, but then... nothing. Sickening is what it is. Look, there's not much we can do down here. I'm going to tote this lot upstairs, where it's more comfortable and the lighting's better. This digging through old files is boring, routine police work and, to be frank, It will take days to get through it all, and even more to do the necessary follow-ups and I don't need you looking over my shoulders, so I suggest you—"

"I get it," she said, interrupting him. "There's no need for you to suggest anything. I'll go back to my office and do some digging into the old geological surveys and see if I can come up with anything."

"Yeah, well... That's sounds a lot more productive than watching me work. You do that. I'll do this," he nodded at the stacks of files, "we'll stay in touch. If either of us finds anything... well, you get the idea, right?"

She nodded. "Of course. I'll leave you to it then. Bye, Jack."

"Yeah... Bye," he said. Then, as an afterthought, he said, "It's nice... to meet you, Amelia. Have a good night. Let's talk in the morning. I'll call you, yes?"

"Yes. It was nice to meet you, too," she lied. "You have a good night, too, Jack." And with that, she turned and headed for the elevator, leaving Jack staring after her.

Jack had to make three trips via the elevator to the situation room. He loaded everything onto hand carts—small tables on wheels—and carted everything up to a spare office off the main situation room. And there he unloaded them.

The office was a luxury he wasn't used to, but as it wasn't being used, *what the hell?* he thought as he piled the twenty-eight boxes along the south wall opposite the pair of white boards set against the north wall, following the timeline as laid out in his grandfather's primary log book, starting in 1974 when Mary Ellen Grimes disappeared on her way home from work.

Having unloaded the boxes, he stepped back, stuck his hands in his pant's pockets and stared at them. *Kate's gonna be pissed when she sees this lot,* he thought, gloomily. *One case, she said, just one, but it doesn't work like that, does it, Jack?* He shook his head, turned to the blank white boards, wondering where to begin. It wasn't his first case as lead detective, nor was it his second or third, or even the tenth, but the magnitude of it was... overwhelming. *I need some help.* He pulled a face at the thought. *But that ain't gonna happen!*

Finally, he made up his mind and stepped over to the white boards and began listing the names of the victims according to the timeline.

· Mary Ellen Grimes, 25, April 15, 1974
· Sarah Louise Mitchell, 25, March 3, 1975
· Patricia "Patty" Henderson, 19, June 12, 1975

And so on and so on until, after adding their occupations, both boards were full. *Geez,* he thought, *and I've not put up the first photo yet.*

He heaved a sigh and sat down at the empty desk, set his elbows on the top, rested his chin in both hands and stared at the white boards, then sat up and looked at the boxes and shook his head.

He leaned back in the chair, half closed his eyes, sucked on his bottom lip, lost in thought.

Geez, what the hell was going on up there on the mountain?

Twenty-eight missing people and... nothing. What the hell was granddad up to? He was a good detective... Damn; I wish he was still alive so I could pick his brains. Why did he never mention it to me? He could have. Hell, he should have. I was a detective, after all. Talk about the one that got away. It must have been a huge downer for him.

He opened one of the desk drawers; it was empty. He looked in the others; they were all empty except for one that held a stack of six yellow notepads. He grinned, took one out and spent the rest of the afternoon digging through the files, making notes and lists. By four-forty-five, the desktop was a cluttered mess of manila files and sheets of yellow notepaper. To anyone else, it would have looked like chaos; to Jack... well, it was "organized... chaos."

It was almost five o'clock when Kate stepped into the office and leaned against the doorjamb, her arms folded across her chest.

"So?" she began. "Talk to me, Jack. What the hell are you doing in here, and what the hell's going on?" She nodded at the piles of banker's boxes.

6

Thursday Afternoon

KATE
 5pm

IT WAS ALMOST five o'clock when I stepped into Jack's commandeered office and as I looked around, my heart sank. I sighed, leaned against the doorjamb, folded my arms and stared at him.

"So?" I said, seriously. "Talk to me, Jack. What's going on?" I nodded at the piles of banker's boxes."

"Twenty-eight..." He hesitated. "My grandfather's files. I thought..."

I regarded him skeptically. Then slowly shook my head and said, "That wasn't the plan, was it? You were supposed to look into one set of remains and wait for identification. That was the agreement, was it not? You were told not to expand it into a major investigation until we had something concrete to take to the chief. If he happens by and takes it into his head to look in here, it will be curtains for both of us."

"I know, but..."

"There's always a but with you, Jack, isn't there? Well, what I need you to do is take a step back and wait until we know what we're dealing with."

I stared at him. He shrugged, then said, "You assigned this case to me because of my grandfather's involvement back in the day. What was I supposed to do? He was investigating twenty-eight of the sixty-one missing persons cases. These are his case files. They're..." He paused, glanced at the boxes and then continued. "Look, what was I supposed to do, ignore them? That's not how it works. I can't do that. You know that, Kate."

I did know that, but I wasn't going to agree with him. He was out of line, and that was it. "So what have you found, then?" I asked.

He hesitated for a moment, opened his mouth to speak, then changed his mind and closed it again and stared at me.

"Well?" I asked.

He shrugged, truculently, and replied, "Nothing."

I nodded. It was as I expected. "Right," I said. "So now I want you to step away, leave everything as it is, lock the door, go home and wait for Doc Sheddon to identify the remains, or not. In the meantime, stick to the remains in the cave. I mean it, Jack!"

He glared at me, obviously angry, but, eventually, he nodded and did as I asked. "Bright and early tomorrow, Jack. My office. Okay?"

"Of course, Captain," he muttered, and I smiled as he turned off the lights and locked the door behind us.

"Look, Jack," I said, putting a hand on his arm to stop him from rushing off. "I'll talk to the chief, okay?"

He nodded, obviously unhappy, then turned away and headed for the elevator. Me? I followed him. I had a date with the chief... not literally, of course. I had to make my report.

It went better than I expected. He seemed to have gotten over whatever had been bothering him earlier in the day and was in an almost... jovial mood, which was a good thing, because I'd decided that rather than let Jack get caught stepping out of the box, which I knew he would, I would fill him in on what Jack had found.

"Sixty-one?" he asked, obviously stunned. "Is he sure?"

I nodded. "Jack is one of the best at this kind of thing," I replied. "If he says sixty-one, you can take it to the bank."

He looked thoughtfully at me, then said, "So, how d'you want to handle it, Captain?"

When he called me captain, I knew he was serious. "More to the point, Chief," I said, "how d'you want me to handle it? We're talking serious money, here. And there's bound to be flack from the powers that be. This thing could turn nasty in a hurry."

He gripped his chin between forefinger and thumb while he thought about it; something I hadn't seen him do many times in the past. Then he said, "I can handle the flack, but is North capable of handling something of this magnitude?"

I thought about that for a second or two. "I think he is, but I'll keep a close eye on him and provide backup as needed. And he has a steadying hand in Doctor Amelia Croft, the forensic geologist from UTC."

He nodded, then said, "Let's give him his head, then, and see how it goes. If you think you need to step in and take over, don't hesitate to do so. Keep me informed. Have a good night, Kate."

And that was it. Jack had himself an investigation, but I wasn't going to tell him right away. I decided I'd let him run with it, but keep a very tight rein on him.

Friday Morning

JACK
   9am
   Detective Morton

JACK AND AMELIA agreed to meet for breakfast the following morning at Ruby Sunshine on Market Street. Amelia arrived ten minutes early and Jack—typically—arrived five minutes late.

"Sorry," he said as he sat down opposite her and gestured for the waiter to bring him coffee. "Traffic!" He shrugged. "Not good at this time of day. How are you? You have a good night?"

"Enough with the pleasantries, Jack," she replied. "This is purely a professional relationship." She said. "I know you don't like me and… Well, you're okay, I guess."

Jack grinned at her and said, "Why don't you tell me how you really feel, Amelia? Nobody said I don't like you. In fact, quite the opposite is true. I do agree with you, though, about it being strictly business."

He took a sip of his coffee, then said, "What would you like to eat?"

She pursed her lips, thought for a moment, then said, "Just some toast and marmalade, I think."

He looked at her in surprise, frowning. "Marmalade? Yuk! That all?"

"Yes, I never eat much in the mornings. It makes... Well, never mind. How about you?"

He looked skeptically at her, then looked up and nodded to the waiter. Jack ordered toast and a marmalade for her and pancakes with two eggs over easy for himself.

They ate for the most part in silence until finally Jack pushed his plate away, looked at her and said, "There's not much we can do until they identify the remains, other than research," Jack said. "Kate and my chief are insisting we wait until we ID the victim, so I suggest we spend our time doing what we do best. I'll interview some of my grandfather's persons of interest and you—"

"There's no need for you to bother about me," she said, interrupting him. "I have plenty to do. Let's just agree to stay in touch. How about we agree to talk at the end of the day?"

Jack nodded. "Sure," he said, a little intimidated by her brusqueness. "So, that's it, for now, then?"

She nodded. "Yes, that's it, I think. If I find anything, I'll call you. You do the same."

He nodded. She stood, picked up her phone and keys, and said, "Thank you for breakfast, Jack. It's been nice. Have a good day. Talk to you soon." And with that, she walked away, leaving Jack once again wondering what the hell he'd gotten himself into. *Stuck up*— he pushed the thought away, waved the waiter over for a coffee refill, took out his notebook and read the first name on his list.

"Detective James Morton," he muttered. "Jim. Hmmm." *He's eighty-nine. Geez. Thirty year's service. Retired in 2000. Passed over for promotion seven times. Who the hell's dog did he kick, I wonder? Eighty-frickin'-nine. I hope he still has all his faculties.*

Jack stared into his coffee cup, thinking about the call he'd had that morning. Kate had told him she'd run his findings by the chief and that he was to go ahead and start the interviews with Charlie's contacts, but that was all until they heard from Doc Sheddon.

He heaved a sigh, reached for his wallet, dropped two tens and five on the table, and left.

Twenty minutes later, he was parked outside Detective Jim Morton's front door in Highland Park.

He sat for a moment and looked at his notes. Detective Morton was a dark-skinned Chattanooga native. A Korean War veteran, he joined the police force after his military service. His wife, Helen, died five years ago in 2018. He had two children, both girls, both now in their fifties. He was also Charlie North's long-time partner.

He looked out the window at Morton's front door, then muttered, "Okay, let's do this."

He exited the car, walked to the front door, thumbed the doorbell, and waited.

"It's open," a powerful voice called from somewhere deep inside. "Come on in."

Jack opened the door and walked inside. It was a small, three-bedroom home with a front door that opened into a small, formal living room. He looked around. It was empty.

"Come on through." The voice said.

He nodded to himself and smiled as he walked through into a larger, much more comfortable room to see the man sitting in a large recliner in front of a gas log fire with an aging Jack Russell terrier on his lap. The TV was on just to the left of the fireplace, the remote at hand on the arm of the chair.

The dog looked up at him, tensed, and issued a low growl.

"Easy, girl," Morton said. Then to Jack, "Who the hell are you, as if I couldn't guess?"

"I'm Detective Jack North, Mr. Morton. I'd like to talk to you about—"

"I know what you want to talk about. There's coffee in the kitchen. Go pour yourself some, and pour one for me while you're at it, black with a little sugar." He handed Jack his empty mug, saying, "And wash that out, will you? Sally likes coffee, too, straight from my mug."

Jack grinned down at him, shook his head and did as he was asked, though he refrained from coffee for himself.

He returned from the kitchen and handed the old man his mug, then he sat down on a second recliner in front of him, leaned forward, put his elbows on his knees, and clasped his hands together in front of him.

"So," Morton said, "you caught my old case, huh?"

"How did you know that's why I'm here?" Jack asked.

Morton shrugged. "It was only a matter of time. I'm just glad I lived long enough to see it reopened. What d'you have so far?"

"Not much," Jack replied, leaning forward, his hands clasped together in front of him. "Just some bones we found in Forrest's Cave that we have yet to identify. I know you and Charlie were investigating some twenty-eight missing persons cases. Well, that number is up to sixty-one now, by the way. Why don't you tell me your story, Mr. Morton? Is it okay if I record the interview?"

Morton nodded as Jack took a small digital recorder from his pocket and turned it on.

"Sure," he said, then frowned, did something strange with the corners of his mouth, and twisted them into a grimace.

He was quiet for a moment, his weathered hands trembling slightly as he stared down into the dark liquid.

Was he seeing reflections of a past he'd spent decades trying to forget? Jack didn't know, but he waited patiently, watching the old man wrestle with memories.

"Mary Ellen Grimes was the first," he began. "She disappeared in 1974," Morton said, finally. "I was thirty-nine, and I thought I knew everything. I thought being a detective was about finding the truth." He laughed, bitterly. "Boy, was I ever mistaken…?" He paused.

"Give me a minute," he said as he put the mug on the side table to his left and then gently pushed the dog off his lap and rose slowly from the recliner, pulling a face as he did so. He was obviously feeling his age. He shuffled over to the fireplace, took a key from the mantlepiece, then went to a locked cabinet on the far side of the room, and shakily inserted it into the lock and opened both doors to reveal stacks of notebooks and manila folders, their edges yellow with age.

"These are my personal records," he said. "I started noticing things that didn't add up right from the start," he continued, pulling out a weathered notebook. "Mary Ellen's car; we found it behind the Brass Register where she worked. Her purse was still inside, everything neat as you please. Too neat. And that witness, the one who saw her talking to someone in a nice suit? Gone within a week. Left town, they said. Never saw him again."

"D'you have a name?" Jack asked.

Morton flipped through the pages, then looked at him, a sly smile on his lips. "Joe Smith," he said. "Obviously fake. We tried to run him down, but he was gone with the wind, so to speak."

Morton's fingers flipped through the faded pages of his notebook, filled with cramped handwriting and coded notes. "It was the frickin' Caldwells," he muttered. "I know it was."

He turned and looked down at Jack. "You have a partner, sonny?"

"No, well, not really. My captain is insisting I work with a forensic geologist, a Doctor Amelia Croft."

"That's good," the old man said, "very good."

Then, before Jack could ask him why it was good, he continued, "You need to look at the Caldwells… You know who they

49

are, right?" he asked as he returned to his chair and sat down heavily.

Jack nodded. "They own a mining and minerals company, Cornerstone... If I remember correctly. They also own several gravel quarries... and—"

"And most of the caves on the mountain," Morton interrupted him. "Not Ruby Falls, though. That's another enterprise entirely; completely legit. That entire mountain, all the way down through Alabama, is riddled with caves and caverns. Most people don't know that only three miles of it are in Tennessee, that it stretches ninety miles from Chattanooga all the way to Gadsden. Cornerstone owns the mineral rights to most of it, or at least they did. That damn company was worth almost a billion dollars when I retired back in 2000. God only knows what they're worth today."

He paused, then continued. "I was convinced—still am—that the Caldwells were behind the disappearances: all twenty-eight of them."

"I know," Jack said. "I have my grandfather's files. You were his partner. Charlie North."

Morton stared wide eyed at Jack, then nodded. "Your name," he said. "I should have known. Well, well. Now there's a coincidence... or is it?"

Jack shook his head. "No, it's why I was assigned the case. They're excavating Forrest's Cave. As I said, they found a body. Well, a skeleton. I caught the case because of the connection."

The old man's eyes lit up. "It's happening then. The circle is complete. The caves are giving up their dead. What you have is only the first."

"Sixty-one," Jack said.

Morton stared at Jack, then shook his head and whispered, "Sixty-one? That's..." He trailed off, seemingly lost for words.

Jack nodded, then said, "Yeah, sixty-one. But please, continue your story."

The old man sat down again and leaned back in his chair and

the dog jumped up on his lap. He caressed its ears as he gathered his thoughts. "Every lead we had pointed to the Caldwells—it was all in the files. But what little evidence we had disappeared: everything that might've mattered... all gone. Photos, statements, physical evidence... gone. And then the pressure started."

He fell silent, lost in his memories. Jack watched him silently. He could see the weight of it all in the slope of his shoulders, the haunted look in his faded blue eyes.

"Chief called us in three times that final week," he continued. "The first time it was friendly - just suggestions about where our time might be better spent. The second time, it was not so friendly. The third time..." He shook his head. "Well, he mentioned Charlie's kids by name. Talked about our pensions. The message was clear enough."

He paused again, then looked at Jack and said, "My partner, Charlie North... Well, well. He wouldn't let it go, you know? He kept pushing, asking questions. He told me he found out something, too, though he never told me what it was. They forced him to take early retirement. We kept in touch over the years, but I figured someone must have gotten to him, because he never spoke of the case to me again, nor to anyone else as far as I knew.
"

He laid his chair back and stared at the flames, and again, he appeared to be lost in thought. Then, quite suddenly, he sat up, and for a moment the years fell away, revealing the young detective who, with his partner, first caught this case. "You want to know what really happened to Mary Ellen Grimes? Start with the cave. We were all looking at the wrong thing - the car, the restaurant, the witnesses. But I think it was about the cave. Always was."

He pushed the dog off his lap and stood up again and went back to the cabinet. He reached inside and pulled out a folded map, its creases worn nearly through. "I spent years marking every cave entrance, every mine shaft, every place they might've...

might've used to get rid of the bodies. Charlie was close to something in those caves. A few weeks before he died, he told me he'd found a connection between the Caldwells' mining operations and an entire network of unmapped tunnels. See?"

His hands shook as he spread the map out on the coffee table. "I tried to warn those researchers back in '94 when they started poking around the same areas. Charlie had been officially retired a couple of years or so then. But they didn't listen. Nobody ever listened."

He looked up at Jack. His eyes were sharp, the look on his face urgent. "You've got what we, Charlie and me, never had, a partner who knows those caves, knows how to read their stories. Don't make our mistakes. Don't go at this head-on. They've had sixty years to perfect their operation, to bury their secrets. And they're still out there, still watching."

He glanced quickly at the window, then back again at Jack, an almost unconscious movement. "Be careful who you trust. The department's not the same as it was in my day, but money still talks. And the Caldwells... they've had generations of practice at making problems disappear."

Jack nodded, frowning, not quite knowing what to make of grandfather's onetime partner.

"I'll keep it in mind," he said.

"That's it, Jack," he said, standing upright. "That's all I have. As I said, they're always watching, so you'd better go now."

Jack rose to his feet. Morton came around the coffee table and grabbed his hand in both of his. His grip was surprisingly strong. "One more thing before you go," he said, still holding his hand. "That night, the night before Mary Ellen disappeared, she called the station. 'Nothing urgent,' she said. She just wanted to report something strange she'd seen at work, at the Brass Register. The desk sergeant told her to come by in the morning. She never made it. The record of that call... it disappeared from the logs. But I remember. I remember everything."

Jack thanked him for his time, and the map, told him he'd be in touch, and then left him standing there, his back to the fire, his dog at his feet. It was just after twelve noon.

Back in his car, Jack sat back and closed his eyes. The interview had been productive; more than productive, and he was surer than ever that he was onto something, something big.

The Caldwell's, he thought. *Was Charlie really onto something? Why did he never talk about the case? Why did he take early retirement? Was it forced upon him? Who was the chief back then, I wonder? I should have asked Morton. Never mind. I'll find out easy enough. Yeah, that's what I'll do.*

Friday Afternoon

Chief Hargrove

2pm

It was just after twelve thirty when Jack arrived back at the police department on Amnicola Avenue. He parked out front and went into the lobby and looked at the photos on the walls of the past and present chiefs of police.

There he is, Chief Robert Hargrove, 1960 to 1980.

He looked at his watch. *Twelve-forty-two. Good. They should all be at lunch by now.*

He swiped himself through and took the elevator to the situation room, went to his desk, opened up his computer, and did a quick search.

"Hah," he muttered. "There he is, the Paradise Gardens Assisted Living. I know where that is."

The ride to the facility just off Hixson Pike in North Chattanooga took a little less than twenty minutes, and Jack arrived almost exactly at two o'clock.

The Paradise Gardens assisted living facility belied its name. It was one of those places where Chattanooga's elderly wait out their final years in sterile comfort. Chief Robert Hargrove, once the most powerful law enforcement officer in the city, now occupied Room 237, his world reduced to a hospital bed and a window overlooking the parking lot.

At ninety-five, his body was failing him. Fortunately, his mind remained razor sharp.

After checking in at reception, Jack knocked gently on the door, opened it and stepped inside.

The old man was lying propped up in bed with his eyes closed. The TV was on, but the sound was turned off. All that was to be heard was the sound of the oxygen tube in his nose hissing softly.

"Sit down," Hargrove whispered without opening his eyes. "Who are you and what d'you want?"

Jack sat down beside the bed. "I'm Detective Jack North with the Chattanooga PD," he replied. "I want to talk to you about the events of 1970 to 1989 when you retired, sir."

His eyes snapped open. He turned his head slightly to look at him. He studied him for a moment with rheumy eyes that still could command attention.

"Charlie North's boy?"

Jack shook his head. "No, sir. His grandson."

"Good man, Charlie," he said. "I mistreated him. Wish I could do it over."

"What can you tell me about it, Chief?" Jack asked, not really knowing what else to say.

"I figured someone would come eventually," he said, his voice barely above a whisper. "I saw the news about the cave. About what they found." He adjusted his position slightly, the movement causing him to wince. "You've got Charlie's old files, don't you? Of course you do. The man always was too thorough for his own good."

Hargrove's gnarled fingers gripped the bed rail; whether from physical pain or memory, Jack couldn't tell.

"You want to know why I did it," he said. It was a statement rather than a question. "Why I called him and Morton to my office and warned 'em off. Why I transferred Morton before he got himself killed." He laughed bitterly; the laugh turned into a coughing fit. When it subsided, there was blood on the tissue he was holding to his mouth. "It wasn't just about money, though God knows there was plenty of that."

He gestured weakly toward a photo on the nightstand of a much younger Hargrove shaking hands with a man Jack knew to be Edwin Caldwell at some charity function. "You have to understand what Chattanooga was back then," he continued. "The power structure. The rules. Caldwell didn't just run the mines, he ran everything. City council, judges, banks... Even the damned churches answered to him."

Hargrove's voice strengthened as he delved into the past. "That night, after Mary Ellen Grimes disappeared, Edwin called me personally. Not in his usual way. He usually had intermediaries for... making arrangements. But this was different. He was scared. He said the girl had overheard something. Something big. Bigger than the usual payoffs and permit fixing."

He stopped, looked at Jack, squinting, studying his face. "You found something in those caves, didn't you? Something that explains why he was so scared?"

Jack nodded but remained silent, letting the old man talk.

"I told myself I was protecting the department," he said, winging. "Protecting the city. You shut down Caldwell's operations, you shut down half of Chattanooga." He laughed again. It sounded hollow. "Petty little lies we tell ourselves, don't we? Truth is, I was protecting myself. My pension. My family. My reputation."

He reached for a cup of water with shaking hands. "Charlie was right about the caves. Morton, too. They knew there was something there, something that connected it all. A week before Charlie retired, Morton came to me. He said Charlie'd found proof of what the Caldwells were really doing in those caves and that he wanted to take it federal. I called Edwin before Morton even left my office. He said he'd fix it, and he did. I don't think Charlie was ever the same after what they did to him. Biggest regret of my life. I should've listened to Morton, but I didn't. Instead..."

"What did they do to him?" Jack asked.

"I don't know. I didn't want to know. Threatened his family, probably..."

He trailed off, staring at the photo. "You know what the real hell is, Detective North? I never even knew exactly what they were doing in those caves. I never wanted to know. I just kept taking the money, giving the orders, looking the other way. But sometimes... sometimes late at night, I can hear them. All of them, the ones I helped bury. All the ones I failed."

He turned back to look at Jack, suddenly urgent. "Check the department's building maintenance logs from '74 to '82. Under my signature. Requisitions for 'special equipment.' Cave gear. Diving equipment. Things a police department had no business ordering. Follow that trail. I kept copies... insurance, I told myself. But I never had the guts to use them."

The oxygen machine beeped, and Hargrove sank back into his pillows, exhausted. "One more thing," he whispered. "May 3rd, 1982. I ordered a records purge. Routine procedure, I called it. But there was nothing routine about what we destroyed that day. Except... except I had my secretary, Alice Kendrick, make copies first. She should still have them. Sweet woman, Alice. Retired to Florida years ago. Never married. Still sends me Christmas cards. Talk to Alice. Tell her I said sorry. Tell her I said it was okay for her to give them to you. "

He closed his eyes. "That's all I can give you, Detective. Not enough to make up for what I did. What I allowed to happen. But maybe... maybe it will help you finish what your grandfather and Morton started." He closed his eyes, heaved a heavy sigh, and seemed to relax. "Maybe I can get myself right with God now... before I go," he muttered, so quietly Jack could barely hear him.

"Thank you, sir," Jack said as he stood up and prepared to leave.

Hargrove opened his eyes and said, "They're still out there, you know. The ones who followed me as chief. The ones who took the same deals, made the same choices. Be careful who you trust, Detective. The caves... they're not the only things in Chattanooga with dark secrets."

Jack looked at him. He was serious. He could tell.

Hargrove waved his hand dismissively and looked away.

Jack pursed his lips, shook his head, and left.

ALICE KENDRICK. He thought as he sat in his car outside the facility. *I wonder.*

First, he checked his watch. *It's almost three-fifteen. If I leave by four, with the time change—it's two-fifteen there—I can be in Fort Walton by... Hmm, it's five-and-a-half hours so, hah. I can be there by eight. If I can see her tonight—*

He took out his phone, asked Siri for the number, then he called Alice Kendrick. After a short conversation with her, hung up the phone grinning, drove the five miles to his apartment, ran to his bedroom, packed an overnight bag, and walked quickly out the door. Ten minutes later, his cruise control set at seventy-five, he was on I-24 heading west to I-59 and from there to Fort Walton Beach, Florida.

Friday Evening

ALICE KENDRICK

8:05pm

JACK SMILED AS HE DROVE, thinking about what he was doing. *Geez, Kate will have a conniption when she finds out what I've done. There's no way in hell she's going to pay for the trip, but what the hell, it's maybe a hundred bucks for gas and thirty for a cheap room, if I decide to stay.*

He turned on the radio and settled in for the drive.

Four and a half hours later, he crossed the Alabama Florida line and stopped for gas and a pee break. That done, he grabbed a giant Snickers bar and an energy drink from the gas station convenience store and ten minutes after he'd stopped; he was on his way again.

Ten miles out, he called Alice.

"Alice?" he asked when she answered. "It's Jack North. I'm maybe fifteen minutes out."

"Come in the back way," Alice Kendrick said. "Fewer prying eyes and fewer cameras that way."

"Got it," Jack replied. "See you in a few minutes."

"I'll have coffee ready," she said and hung up.

He arrived at the Pelican Bay retirement home at five after eight, still smiling to himself.

Alice's unit at Pelican Bay looked like any other Florida retirement home unit... from the outside—pink stucco, white trim, and carefully tended roses. But inside? Now that was another story. Hers was almost an office with a bedroom, a private archive. Banker's boxes lined the walls of the living room, each labeled with precise handwriting. A modern scanner and computer sat on a desk beside a vintage Rolodex. Alice, herself, was a diminutive lady. No more than five-three with silver hair and sparkling blue eyes. She was, Jack knew, seventy-nine, but she didn't look a day over sixty.

"How did you manage all this?" Jack asked, awed.

"Just like Johnny Cash sang, one piece at a time." She almost giggled, but she didn't. "This shouldn't take too long," she said. "I have everything ready for you. Are you staying over or going straight back?"

"That depends on how long this takes," Jack replied.

"As I said, not long. Would you like some coffee?" she asked

"Oh hell ye—" He grimaced, corrected himself and said, "Sorry, yes, ma'am, please."

"Don't call me that," she said as he followed her into the kitchen. "My name is Alice. Bob always called me that. You can, too. How is he, by the way?"

"Okay, I guess. He was in bed when I saw him so—"

"Yes, yes," she said as she slipped a pod into the coffeemaker and set it going. "I know. He's failing, bless him. Milk? Sugar? He isn't a bad man, you know."

"Black, please ma... Alice. You don't seem surprised I'm here," he said as she handed him the steaming cup.

"Forty years as a police secretary; why would I be surprised?" she said. "I started at the PD when I was nineteen and worked my way up the ladder. I was secretary to two chiefs, Bob, then John Hart. You learn to keep everything." Her silver hair was perfectly styled, her movements easy, almost graceful, as she pulled on a pair of cotton archival gloves. "Most people underestimate secretaries. Think we're just coffee and typing. But we see everything. Hear everything. And, most important, we remember everything."

She picked up a leather-bound ledger from a pile of files on the table. "May 3rd, 1982. I remember every minute of that day. Bobby—Chief Hargrove—called me in early. He said we had to purge some files. 'Routine,' is what he said, but his hands were shaking."

Alice handed the ledger to him. He opened it, took one look, then closed it again. It was all gobbledygook to him, so he laid it down on the table as she spread the contents of a thick manila envelope across her desk in separate piles.

"These," she said, her hand on the first pile, "are Charlie North's original case notes along with detailed witness statements from the Brass Register's staff, tire track analysis and photos at a cave entrance, a list of suspicious vehicles near the crime scene, and the connection between disappearances and mining company board meetings.

"In this pile are the crime scene photos: Mary Ellen's car, showing signs of professional cleaning, footprints leading into the cave entrance, suspicious tire tracks, strange markings on cave walls, and evidence of recent cave modifications

"And in this pile we have financial records: weekly payments from Caldwell Mining to security consultants, bonuses to specific police officers, property transfers to police officials and," she looked up at him, "offshore account numbers.

"Finally," she said, "these are the patrol logs, records of the officers reassigned from cave area, unusual shift changes, missing time periods, changed patrol routes."

She looked at him and smiled. "See these notations?" she said, pointing to tiny marks in the margins. "My codes. Here's the key." She handed him a small, slim black notebook. "Names, dates, connections. I had to be careful. One never knew who might find these."

She stepped over to a filing cabinet and pulled out more folders. "It wasn't just the Grimes case. Every time someone disappeared, the same pattern. Files would vanish. Officers were transferred. Witnesses changed their stories. This one almost got me killed. It's a report about cave maintenance work the night Mary Ellen Grimes disappeared. Someone went through my desk drawers after I copied it. Next day, my brakes failed. It was pure luck I survived."

She looked intently at him, like a giant bird of prey. "You want to know why I'm still alive? Because I made sure they knew these records would surface if anything happened to me. Dead man's switch, it's called these days, I believe. Back then, we just called it insurance."

She went to her computer and pulled up dozens of files of scanned copies. "Everything's digitized now. And I made multiple backups. Some in places even the Caldwells can't reach." She turned to look at him, and her face softened as she said, "I've been waiting for someone like you, Detective. Someone who'd actually look at the evidence instead of burying it."

She handed him a USB drive. "It's all there. A complete copy. But the originals stay here. I still don't trust the department, no offense, but there are still too many of the old guard still around. But you, you wouldn't be here if Bob hadn't sent you. Too many people with too much to lose, Detective. I hope that won't put you off."

Jack looked at her, smiled at her, then said, "Damn, lady. I wish you were still around today. I don't know what to say. You..."

You... You're amazing. Don't worry. We're going to bring them down, whatever it takes. You have my word. We done here?"

"Yes," she replied, smiling up at him. "One more thing. Check the blueprints for the Mountain City Club. Make sure they're the real ones, from 1940. Look at the tunnel markings. It might explain how they moved things—and people—around without being seen."

He nodded. "Thank you, Alice. I think I love you."

"Oh, get out of here, you silly boy," she said, smiling, obviously pleased by what he'd said.

At the door, she straightened her shoulders and said, "Bobby Hargrove wasn't a bad man. Just a weak one. But weakness can do as much damage as evil. Maybe more."

"And the original files?" Jack asked.

"They'll be here, God willing, if and when you need them. And Detective? Be very careful. You're dealing with some very bad and powerful people."

Back in his car, he looked at his watch. It was nine forty. He did a quick calculation on his fingers, checked the gas level; it was showing the tank was a quarter full—*Hmm, if I leave now I could be home by three in the morning.* He blew air out through his teeth, thought about it for a moment—*well, the roads will be clear if nothing else*—then made his decision. *Hell, I don't want to waste the weekend down here. I'm going home.*

Sunday Morning

JACK

   10am

   Jack's Apartment

IT WAS ten minutes to three when Jack arrived back at his home that Sunday morning, wiped out and so ready for bed. So tired was he, he set the alarm for nine o'clock and simply stripped down and crawled under the covers.

Strangely enough, he had a relatively dreamless night. He woke to the sound of the alarm at nine o'clock, somewhat refreshed, but with his back aching and a knot in his left thigh muscle.

He went to the bathroom and turned on the shower—cold— and stepped in, totally unphased by the shock of the cold water, something he'd grown used to over his years as a cop. And there he stood for several minutes before turning up the heat almost to scalding and let the water play through multiple jets onto his back and legs, easing his aches and pains.

Ten minutes, two arthritis Tylenol pills, a quick shave and his teeth vigorously brushed, he dressed in blue jeans and a white T-shirt and went to the kitchen where he made himself some coffee and toast and then went to the living room.

Jack stood just inside the door, a cup of coffee in one hand and a plate of buttered toast in the other, and shook his head. His living room looked like a war room. Papers covered every inch of his oversize dining table that took up most of the free space. Papers connected by red strings that crisscrossed above the table like a spider's web.

He slid Alice's USB drive into a port on his air-gap laptop, an old habit from his cybercrime rotation

"Yikes... Oh, geez," he muttered as he studied one patrol log after another from 1974 through 1980. The reassignments around the caves weren't random. Each time someone disappeared, the same pattern emerged: experienced officers were pulled away and rookies assigned; rookies who wouldn't know what to look for. He recognized some of the names, men who'd risen quickly through the ranks. Men still in power.

We've got to secure this, he thought. He sat for a minute, wondering what to do. Then he nodded to himself, emailed Amelia, attached the files, all of them, hesitated for a moment, then clicked send.

Less than ten minutes later, his phone buzzed. It was Amelia.

"Good morning," he said. "You busy?"

"I got your email and the files. My God, what's going on?"

"I don't know. Hargrove's secretary handed me this pile of.... I haven't had time to look at it all yet. Did you look at the Mountain City Club like I asked?"

"I did," she replied. "The official maps are wrong. The original surveys show at least three major passages that were deliberately left off. And Jack? They connect directly to the Mountain City Club basement."

"That's what Kendrick said—she was Robert Hargrove's secretary—only she thought there were only two. What about the geological samples I gave you? The ones Charlie collected?"

"I'll have them analyzed as soon as I can," she replied. "Off-book. I have a friend at Georgia Tech who owes me a favor. She'll do it, and she knows to keep quiet. What are you thinking, Jack?"

"Right now, I'm not thinking much about anything. I just got back from Florida at three this morning. I need coffee and something to eat. Kate… I mean Captain Gazzara said we're to lie low until we have an identification on the bones you guys found. I have to stay within bounds. I'll be in enough trouble when she finds out what I've been doing. You want to come over and help me go through these files?" he asked as he wandered over to his kitchen window and looked out at the street below, a habit he'd picked up early in his career, one that had served him well.

He spotted a black SUV parked at the corner. There was smoke coming from the exhaust. *The engine's running,* he thought. *Hmm, could be nothing. Maybe not.*

"I'm not sure that would be wise, Jack," she replied. "Considering the instructions you've been given."

"Yeah, you're probably right," he replied. "But we need to do something with this stuff… to protect it. All of it. If anything happens to…" He trailed off, watching the SUV. "You should make copies, lots of them. D'you have a safe deposit box?"

"I do."

"Then you should put a copy there, and—"

"I get it, Jack. But you're late to the altar," Amelia interrupted him. "I've already sent copies to three universities' secure archives. Time-locked. I miss my weekly check-in, and they go public."

Jack smiled. *The woman thinks like a cop.*

"That's… good thinking," he said, thoughtfully. "I have a lot of paper here. I need to scan it all and put it in a safe place, though where that would be, I don't know."

"What's wrong with the police department? Surely—"

"Hah, are you kidding me?" He laughed. "Take a look at that ledger. See how many cops were on the take. You think anything's changed? That's the last place they need to be, though I will give Kate a copy. She needs to be kept in the loop."

"Can she be trusted?" Amelia asked.

"Seriously? Yes, she can be trusted. So can the rest of her team, and we may have to call on them before this is over." He paused for a second, then continued, "Damn! We need that identification. Whew... Okay, I'm going to scan all this paper and encrypt the files. You have a good weekend. I'll check in with Kate on Monday morning and then call you."

"All right," she said. "I'll talk to you Monday, then." And she hung up, leaving Jack staring at the SUV.

And so it begins, he thought.

He spent the next two hours scanning everything and encrypting the files, then he uploaded them to multiple secure locations. Finally, when all was complete, he sealed the originals in evidence bags, and dated and signed them. Might as well stick to protocol, even if I don't trust the evidence room. *Now a trip to the bank and put a data drive in the safe deposit box*, he thought. He looked at his watch. *Damn! It's after twelve. The bank's already closed. It will have to wait till Monday. In the meantime...* He looked around, smiled took a tiny Ziplock baggy from a kitchen drawer, slipped the drive inside, sealed it closed, then opened the fridge door, took out a pot of Mayo, and pushed the baggy deep into the pot. He made sure the baggy was covered, shook the pot a little to even it out, then screwed on the lid and set it back in the fridge right at the front and closed the door.

I'll take it to the bank Monday morning, he thought. *One the department doesn't know about. Geez, this is ridiculous.*

He sat down at the air-gap laptop and pulled up the files. He wasn't bothered about anybody hacking it, or breaking into it. They would need the encrypted password and his thumbprint to get into it. Five wrong tries and the computer would automatically self-erase everything on it.

He pulled up the financial records. They told their own story of corruption in high places. Weekly payments from Caldwell Mining to "security consultants" that were actually police officials. Property transfers. Offshore accounts. And most damning of all, bonuses paid out days after each disappearance. Some of the recipients were still collecting their police pensions.

At two o'clock that afternoon, he began to record his video deposition. "My name is Detective Jack North. The date is..." He included everything, the records, his conclusions, names and dates, everything, then "If you're seeing this, the chances are I'm dead, but the evidence, all of it, is real. And it all leads back to the Caldwells and the caves."

Finally, at almost six that evening, he called his FBI contact, a woman who'd helped him twice before to crack cases during his stint in Finance. "Sorry to bother you this late on a Saturday," he said when she picked up. "But I need to do this. Remember when you said I'd never run into anything bigger than the Martinez case? Well, how wrong you were. I'm sending you some encrypted files. File them away. If anything happens to me, you'll find the encryption key in a safe deposit box in—" And he gave her the name of the bank and the number of the box. Then, for the next several minutes, he stoically fended off her questions, telling her that all would be revealed at the proper time, and that she was part of his insurance.

He smiled as they talked. He could almost see her shaking her head as she tried to persuade him to bring her in, but all he would say was that his investigation involved Forrest's Cave and some pretty high-flying individuals.

He was again standing at the window when he hung up. The SUV was still there. He bit his bottom lip and turned again to his computers. Fifty years of corruption, murder, and cover-ups, all preserved by a secretary who understood the power of paperwork. Now he just has to live long enough to put it to good use.

The black SUV wasn't there on Sunday, nor was it there when Jack left for work on Monday morning. He slipped into his shoulder rig, checked his Glock, remembering what Alice Kendrick had told him: "Be careful. You're dealing with some very bad and powerful people."

He smiled to himself. It was time to turn on some lights.

11

Monday, November 20, 2023

KATE
8:30am
Kate's Office

JACK ARRIVED at my office door early on Monday morning and I could tell immediately that he had a lot on his mind.

"Looks like you had one hell of a weekend," I said, dryly, as he stepped inside. "Want to tell me about it?"

He flopped down in the chair in front of my desk, looked at me, and said, "You're going to be pissed."

I resisted the urge to shake my head. Instead, I leaned back in my chair, coffee mug in hand, and said, "What the hell have you done this time?"

He smiled sheepishly at me. Then began, "First, on Friday afternoon, I interviewed retired Chief Hargrove."

I stared at him, wondering when the shit from my chief was going to hit the fan. You don't interview a senior officer, retired or not, without an officer of equal rank present and, other than Wesley Johnston, we didn't have such an officer, and I had no doubt Johnston would be on my case as soon as Hargrove called it in, if he hadn't already. But Jack must have read my mind.

"It's okay," he said. "He was okay with it. In fact, he unloaded." He put a thumb drive on my desk. "I recorded the interview. That's a copy..." he paused, hesitated, then continued, "I also interviewed his secretary, Alice Kendrick. That's on the drive, too."

He put his thumb to mouth and nibbled on the nail, obviously at a loss as to what to say next.

"Go on," I said, "What next?"

"I had to drive to Fort Walton to interview her."

I stared at him. "You did *what?*"

He shrugged but didn't answer.

"Am I going to have to drag it out of you, Jack?" I snapped.

He sighed, shook his head and said, "Nope." Then he thought for a moment and continued, "Kate, you have no idea what was going on back then. This case is huge—"

"Wait! What did you just say?" I said. "Did I not tell you to stick to the bones until they were identified?"

"Yes, but—"

"No buts," I snapped. "The chief will—"

"Please, just check this out before you go ballistic on me."

He leaned forward and placed another USB drive on my desk. I stared at it. "What's that?"

"It's all of Hargrove's deleted files. It was him who sent me to see Kendrick... Well, he didn't actually send me, but he told me what she had, and that she would... so I went. Anyway, he told me he'd ordered her to purge everything, which she did, but she kept the originals and took them with her when she retired to Florida. She made copies of everything for me." He nodded at the USB drive. "That's them. Stick it in your computer and take a look-see."

I leaned over and picked up the drive and inserted it in one of the USB ports, opened it, and was confronted by almost five dozen folders.

I looked at Jack. He made a face and shrugged.

The files were all labeled. I clicked on one labeled Financials. It opened, and I began to read through the more than five hundred pages. I didn't need to read through more than two of them before I realized what I had was a ledger containing evidence of widespread corruption in the police department from 1970 through 1984 when Robert Hargrove retired. Recorded therein were payments to officers—senior and patrol—city and county government officials, security officers, and God only knew who else.

I closed the file and made a copy of the contents of the USB drive to my computer, then took a fresh drive from the desk drawer and made a fresh copy. Then I handed Jack his original.

He shook his head. "That one's for you," he said. "I have plenty, all stored away in safe places. If anything happens to me, it all goes public."

"What you have here is potentially dynamite," I said, "but, as it stands, as far as I can tell, there's no direct links between payee and payer, just an amount paid to the payee on such-and-such a date, but not by whom. Obviously I haven't had time to go through it all, but it would seem to me that most of the payees are either dead or retired."

"True," he replied. "I didn't go all the way through that ledger either, but it's just one file out of sixty. What the hell d'you think is on the rest of them? I went through a couple. There are police logs, records of transfers, incident reports, investigation reports. I mean, it seems to me there's a complete record of fourteen years of department activity in those files."

That's what it looked like to me, too, but I was also convinced it was of little use, other than to expose corruption within the department on a wide scale. How it was going to help Jack with his investigation, which was at that time still up in the air, I didn't know.

"And there's another thing, Jack," I said. "The statute of limitations has run out on everything except murder."

He shrugged, but didn't answer.

"Have you spoken of this to anyone else?" I asked.

He looked guilty. "Yeah, I spoke to Amelia Croft… and I gave her a copy of the USB drive."

I took a deep breath, shook my head, and said, "Big mistake, Jack. We don't know if we can trust her."

"I think we can," he said. "She told me she'd locked copies of it away at three different universities, on time locks. If she doesn't check in on time every week, bammo, they go public."

I leaned back in my chair, thinking. *What the hell have we gotten into? I can't go to the chief with it, not yet. He would pitch a fit at what Jack's done. Probably fire him. Me, too. I need to keep it under wraps for now.* I sucked on my lower lip, then made up my mind.

"Okay," I said. "Here's how it is. This, all of it, stays between you and me. At least for now. We wait for the bones to be identified, as we were instructed to do. You have more interviews to carry out, yes?"

He nodded.

"Then you can go ahead with those until we get a positive ID," I said, sternly, "or not, and liaise with Dr. Croft. In the meantime, I'll go through as much of this mess as I can. Understood?"

Again, he nodded.

"We say nothing about Hargrove," I continued, "unless he registers a complaint, which we'll deal with if and when, and we say nothing about your trip to Florida and interview with… what was her name?" I looked at him.

"Alice Kendrick," he replied.

"Alice Kendrick, right," I said. "We'll keep her out of it, too."

He stared at me, then blew air out through his pursed lips, making a noise like a horse whickering.

"If you say so, Cap," he said, a little reluctantly, I thought. "So, what d'you want me to do now?"

"I told you," I said. "All this... it never happened. You go about your investigation of the bones according to your grandfather's records. I'll get in touch with Doc and see if he has a result. If not, I'll hurry him up. Then we'll take it from there. You good with that?"

"Yeah, I guess," he replied. "You'll let me know as soon as..." He trailed off.

"Yes," I said. "I'll let you know. Now get out of here. Keep me in the loop. Got it?"

He nodded, got to his feet, and walked to the door. He put his hand on the knob, then turned and looked at me, his eyebrows raised.

I nodded, and he opened the door and left without another word.

Me? I reached for the desk phone and called Doc Sheddon.

"Good morning, Kate," he said when he answered. "I suppose you want to know if we've ID'd the bones found in Forrest's Cave."

Geez, he can be so annoying sometimes, I thought.

"That's right," I replied. "What d'you have for me?"

"Well, it's preliminary, but yes, we have an ID. Female, young, aged between seventeen and twenty-one. Died of blunt force trauma to the occipital. Someone hit her very hard. There are also what look like defensive wounds to the carpals, metacarpals, and the ulna of the right hand and arm, made by a large knife wielded by a left-handed assailant, in my opinion. So you have a homicide on your hands, and you're looking for at least two assailants. And yes, we were able to match her dental records. She's Mary Ellen Grimes."

"Thanks, Doc," I said. "You'll send me the report?"

"When it's complete, of course," he replied. "Don't I always?"

"That you do, Doc," I said. "I'm most grateful." And with that, I hung up.

I made a note of the name, entered it into the missing persons database and, sure enough, up it came. Mary Ellen Grimes, age 19, disappeared April 15, 1974. *Damn!* I thought. *Now the shit will really hit the fan.*

I picked up the phone and called Jack. Fortunately, he was still on the property, so I had him come back to my office and reluctantly gave him the news.

I expected him to smile. It was his trademark, always cheery Jack North. But this time, he wasn't cheery at all. In fact, he looked downright gloomy, and I could, to some extent, understand why. He was on his own with it, well, on his own except for Dr. Croft and how much use she would be, I had no idea. The problem was, of course, I didn't have the manpower, so he was going to have to go it alone, at least for now.

He dropped into the seat he'd left only a few minutes ago, looked at me and said, "So... Where the hell do we go from here?"

I hated to tell him, but I had no choice. "You're on your own with this one, Jack. I can't spare anybody. What you have here is a single homicide. I have every confidence you can handle it. So get your act together. Don't try to do everything at once. Take it one step at a time. Fortunately, the perps, and most of the witnesses, are either dead or gaga, and you've already interviewed several people. How many d'you have left?"

"That I know of," he said as he pulled out his notebook, "Two, both retired police officers—Sergeant William Cooper and Officer Thomas Henderson—but there may be more now that we know who the victim is. I'll start with them today."

He was silent for a moment, then looked at me and said, "You do realize that this means there could be at least sixty more bodies in that cave, don't you?"

I looked sternly at him. "One thing at a time, Jack!"

He nodded, then said, "Did Doc give you a cause of death?"

"Blunt force trauma to the back of the head. There were also defensive wounds to her right hand and arm, made with a big knife, so he thinks. If it's true, which I'm sure it is—I've never known Doc make a mistake—then we're looking for at least two perps. If you need me, I'm here. I want you to check in with me every morning. I'll help you all I can. I still have to run it by the chief, but that shouldn't be a problem. In the meantime, what we talked about earlier still applies. We'll still keep a lid on it for now."

He nodded, seemed to brighten up a little. "Thanks for the confidence, Kate. I won't let you down."

I smiled at him and said, "I know you won't, Jack."

And I meant it.

Officer Henderson

MONDAY MORNING
10am

JACK WAS, to all intents and purposes, a workaholic, within the restrictions of department overtime protocols, of course. Weekend work was only to be undertaken with the approval of a senior officer. Jack, however, was, as you know, never one to follow the rules. He worked to his own schedule, submitted his paperwork for approval, and was usually unperturbed when it was rejected.

Thus, having finished his enlightening interview with Captain Kate Gazzara, and filled with a new confidence, he decided to begin with Officer Thomas Henderson.

The Rosewood retirement community's recreation room smelled of coffee and disinfectant. Officer Thomas Henderson, now in his eighties, was seated at a small dining table arranging his chess pieces with military precision, his movements deliberate, each piece placed just so. He was a man still seeking order in a world that had stopped making sense to him decades ago.

Jack tapped on the open door and waited.

"Come in," Henderson said without looking up. "Morton called me. You're Charlie North's grandson, right? I've been expecting you."

"That's right," Jack replied. "I'm here—"

"I know why you're here. Sit down. Take a load off."

Jack sat down at the table opposite him. He stared at the old man for a moment, trying to assess him. He looked younger than his eighty-two years. His white hair was cropped short to about a half-inch. His hands were steady; no signs of a shake. His eyes, what he could see of them, were blue. "D'you mind if I record our conversation, Mr. Henderson?"

The old man shook his head and said, "No, go ahead, sonny. There's nothing I'm going to tell you that ain't common knowledge. How old are you?"

Jack looked at him in surprise, frowning. "Thirty-six. Why d'you ask?"

Henderson shrugged. "Just wondered is all. How long have you been a detective?"

"Thirteen years," Jack replied. "Is that important?"

"It could be," he replied. "How come you're still a detective and not a sergeant? You a bad boy, or something?"

Jack smiled at him. "You could say that, I suppose. Not the most popular cop with IA, but I get things done. You were there in 74, weren't you?"

Henderson nodded, then began, "I was just a patrol officer on the mountain back then in 74," he said, not looking up from the chessboard. "There were only six of us. We took turns on nights, walking a beat around the caves. Well, on bikes mostly." His voice was soft with a slight drawl of East Tennessee, worn smooth by years of careful speech. "I hated it. Strange things happened up there at night. Things we were told to ignore."

Jack said nothing. He waited as Henderson moved a pawn, starting a new game against an invisible opponent. The old man's uniform might have been long gone, but the ramrod posture remained, along with the haunted look of someone who'd carried a secret for too long.

"We had… Let's say 'unusual instructions' about the paper-work." He looked up at Jack for the first time. "That's what you want to know about, isn't it?" His eyes were narrowed almost to slits, the corners of his mouth turned down, chin jutted out. It was a look Jack knew well: Henderson had once been a no nonsense, hard-ass policeman.

Jack nodded. Henderson looked down at the chessboard and moved his imaginary opponent's knight.

"We had to log every drunk, every vandal, every teenage couple parking up there. But sometimes, certain vehicles, certain people… Those were different. Those people, we were told to forget. Especially if they were around the mining company's land."

He paused, his fingers hovering over a bishop. "There was this one night in '74. Early spring, end of March, early April. I forget exactly when, but it was just before that Grimes girl went miss-ing. I saw some men carrying something heavy from a truck into one of the maintenance tunnels. Mining company uniforms, sure, but at three in the morning?" He shook his head, glanced at Jack, and then continued. "I called it in, as per procedure."

Henderson's hand trembled slightly as he moved his bishop. "The duty sergeant told me to clear the area, said it was a sched-uled equipment transfer. But I saw that truck again, two weeks later. Different men, same type of… cargo. I wrote it all down, logged every detail." He paused, locked eyes with Jack, then said, "Next morning… my notebook had disappeared from my locker."

"Week after that, I was taken off that beat and transferred to Point Park on the other side of the mountain. Better beat, they said. Easier patrol, more opportunity for advancement. Funny thing about opportunity - sometimes it's just a fancy word for keep your damn mouth shut."

Jack said nothing, content to let the man continue his narrative.

"Cat got your tongue?" Henderson asked, a wry smile on his lips. "Not what you expected, huh?"

Again, Jack didn't reply. Instead, he inclined his head slightly and raised his eyebrows.

Henderson looked again at the game board and continued his silent battle.

"You know, you start noticing patterns after a while. How certain names never appeared in reports. How evidence seems to disappear, just vanish. How witnesses suddenly decide they hadn't seen anything after all. The caves... they weren't just holes in the mountain. They were... hell, I don't know what they were... are."

He tips over his king in defeat, ending the game against himself. "I had enough. I applied to CPD and was lucky enough to get hired, and I quit the Lookout Mountain PD. Last thing I saw up there, just before I left? A black car, expensive. Man in a suit giving orders to some mining company workers. Couldn't hear what was said, but I recognized him. Course I did. Everyone knew Edwin Caldwell; son of a bitch."

He began to reset the chess pieces, each one placed with the same careful precision. "You're gonna get yourself hurt, kid, stirring up old ghosts. Some of us... we've lived with those ghosts a long time. Learned to look the other way, tell ourselves we were just following orders. But the ghosts... they don't care about orders. They just want someone to tell their story. Maybe that's you, Detective. Is it?" He stopped what he was doing with the chessboard and looked up at Jack, a slight smile on his lips.

"I hope so," Jack replied.

Henderson nodded, but remained silent and went back to arranging the board.

"That's it?" Jack asked. "That's all you can remember?"

"Oh I remember, sonny. In my dreams, I remember. Morton, me, your grandfather Charlie, Bill Cooper, we all used to get together once in a while. Charlie was one hell of a cop, so was Jim Morton. How many good people disappeared into those hell holes up there? Nobody knows. Maybe nobody will ever know." He stared at Jack, then continued. "How about you, Detective? Do you have what it takes?" He shook his head and sighed. "I doubt it. Charlie and Jim spent fifteen years trying to figure it out, but they couldn't."

"Maybe I'll get lucky," Jack said, wryly.

"Maybe you will, Jack. Maybe you will." He thought for a moment, then looked past Jack, toward the window. "Check the shift logs for the weeks from April 12, 1974. If they haven't been 'lost' like so much else. I was supposed to patrol the company cave entrance that night, but got called away. Last-minute reassignment, so I was told. I never did know who took my shift. Truth be told, I didn't want to know."

He leaned back in his chair, the chess pieces set ready for a new game, white facing black, order restored. He locked eyes with Jack and said, "That's all I have for you, Detective. I've probably told you more than I should."

He paused again, staring at him, then said, "One last piece of advice: watch your back. Those people don't fool around."

13

Monday afternoon

SERGEANT WILLIAM COOPER
Jack
2pm

IT TOOK A BIT OF DOING, but Jack finally tracked Cooper down, fishing out on Harrison Bay.

Fortunately, the man had his cell phone with him; the number provided by a stoic-looking receptionist on the presentation of his creds and badge. So all it took was a quick twenty-minute drive on Highway 58, and Jack was on the dock waiting for him. He arrived five minutes later in what looked to Jack like an expanded coracle. It was maybe ten feet long by five wide and made of wood with ten horsepower motor on the back.

"Come on, jump in," Cooper said. "I ain't a waistin' no fishin' time talkin' on the dock. I don't get out that often anymore, so come on, and be quick about it."

"Me?" Jack said, his hand on his chest. "You talking to me?"

"Who else would I be talkin' to, damn it? Now either get in the boat or—"

"Geez, is it safe?" He asked as he stepped off the dock. The boat rocked dangerously.

"Sit down, damn it," Cooper said. "Or we'll both be in the water."

Jack sat down on a plank seat in the boat's prow and grabbed the gunwales with both hands.

"There you go," Cooper said, grinning. "Here, put this on." He tossed him a worn life jacket. "Let's go fishin'."

"I'd rather not," Jack muttered, as he struggled into the jacket, conscious of the violent rocking he was causing.

"What was that, sonny?" Cooper asked as he revved the small engine, and the tiny boat did its best to surge forward.

"Nothing," Jack replied.

Five minutes later, they were, by some kind of miracle, anchored twenty feet out from the far shore of the Tennessee River, with one time Sergeant William Cooper casting his rig close to the overhanging, overgrown shrubbery hanging over and into the water.

He was as weathered as was his obviously beloved boat, a man more comfortable with silence than words. At eighty-one, his once-imposing frame had shrunk significantly. He wore a Tennessee Highway Patrol ball cap and what looked to Jack like an antique Colt 1911, .45 in a worn leather holster on his hip. His eyes were sharp, constantly scanning the shoreline as if old habits refuse to die.

"Morton called me. Bin expectin' you, boy," he said without looking at him. He hauled his line in and inspected his empty hook. "I knew your grandad. Good man, he was..." He paused, obviously thinking. "Soon as I heard they found somethin' in that cave," he continued, "I knew it was just a matter of time. Lots of water under the bridge. Not all of it good."

Jack waited while Cooper re-baited his hook, noting how the old sergeant's hands trembled slightly.

"You want to know what Charlie, your grandfather, was all about, don't you? You catch the case? What they found in the cave?"

Jack nodded. "That's about the size of it. I'd also like to know what happened to Mary Ellen Grimes."

"Well, good luck to you, sonny. I don't know what happened to her, but I can guess. They found her, didn't they? That's why you're here. Better stay sharp, them Caldwells ain't people you want to be messin' with."

"You were going to tell me something," Jack said

Cooper looked round at him, his head low, eyes narrowed, squinting to keep out the sun.

"Every Friday night—" Cooper said, before Jack interrupted him.

"If you don't mind, Mr. Cooper, I'd like to record our conversation; for your protection and mine."

"As I was sayin'," he continued, dryly, as he cast his line. "Every Friday night. Same routine. Caldwell and his crowd, the biggies in town, used to meet. They would meet in the big corner booth at the Brass Register. Private like, really. Seven-thirty sharp. Edwin liked punctuality." He adjusted his grip on the rod and tweaked the line. "I was assigned security detail. I think Edwin must have liked me. 'Stand in the corner,' he said. 'look imposin',' he said. 'keep your mouth shut,' he said. Didn't stop me listening, though, did it?"

He was silent for a moment, the river lapping against the boat's hull, a gentle rhythm broken only by the distant hum of the traffic on Highway 58.

"Started in '73. Good assignment, they said. Prestigious. Extra pay." He laughed, shook his head slowly, then continued. "They didn't say what that pay was really for. Not at first, anyway."

He set the rod down, reached beneath his seat, felt around,

then pulled out an old leather-bound notebook, its cover worn, its pages swollen with age. "I started keeping track after the second girl disappeared. Names, dates, conversations. You know, things they said when they thought I was just part of the furniture."

Jack frowned. "That was kind of risky, wasn't it?" he asked. "Weren't they careful with their words?"

"Oh, they were careful all right. Real careful. They never said nothin' that could've... well, you know, anything direct. But you're a cop. You know how it is. You learn to read between the lines, don't you? 'Taking care of problems.' 'Permanent solutions.' 'Underground storage.'" He spit out that last one. "All code words for murder."

He ran his fingers around the edge of the notebook, still on his lap. "I remember the night Mary Ellen disappeared," he said, staring down at the boards. "Edwin called a special meetin'. Not the usual Friday night meetin'. And not at the Brass Register. It was at the Mountain City Club. Emergency meetin', he called it. Oh yeah, Edwin was scared of somethin' all right. I could tell. He was nervous, like. I'd never seen him scared before."

"What was he scared of?" Jack asked.

"The girl knew something, so he said," Cooper replied. "Don't know what. She must've overheard somethin', or saw somethin' she shouldn't have. She worked there at the Brass Register as a waitress. But it was more than that. Edwin said she had proof. Something solid. What it was, though..." He shook his head, still staring at the bottom of the boat. "I don't know what it was." He opened the notebook. The pages crackled. "I made notes that night. Times, names, who came, who left. Two days later," he looked up and locked eyes with Jack, "I got my first overtime envelope."

Jack studied the old man's face. His eyes seemed to droop, his mouth seemed permanently half open. "Why did you keep the notebook if you were taking their money?" he asked.

Cooper smiled. He looked bitter. "Insurance," he said. "It's the reason I'm still alive. I made damn sure they knew I had these notes and that they would go public if anything ever happened to me."

He turned the pages, then held the book up so Jack could see it. "See these names?" he said. "These three tried to retire early. Oh, they retired all right. Permanent retirement, they called it, if you get what I mean. Me?" He wrinkled his nose. "I played it smart. I kept on collectin' my envelopes and kept my mouth shut."

He took a piece of folded paper from between the pages. "This is what you want," he said, looking up at him. "It's the guest list from the club that night. It wasn't just Caldwell and two or three of the others. It was all of them: the city manager. The police chief. Judge Harrison. They was all there, and they were there, and they were all part of what happened." He paused, bit his bottom lip, staring out across the water. "And there was something else. I overheard Edwin talkin' about a tunnel, an old moonshiner's route. It connected the club to the caves. Perfect for moving things, or people, without being seen."

His hand was shaking. "My grandson...," he said, then paused. He's at UTC. Majorin' in engineerin'. He's on a full scholarship from the Caldwell Foundation. Funny how things work out, ain't it? How the past reaches into the present? I've had enough. Let's go in."

He started the boat's motor. "Here, take this notebook," He said as he handed it to him. "I've bin waiting forty years for someone who'd actually use it. You can have it, but just... be careful. The Caldwells might be old money, but their methods ain't so genteel."

As they headed back to the dock, Cooper spoke again. He had to shout to be heard over the motor. "There's one more thing you should know. Check the club's renovation records for '74. They did a lot of work in the club basement that summer. It started right after Mary Ellen disappeared. They poured a lot of concrete, sealed off a lot of areas." As he approached the dock, he cut the motor and let the boat drift. "Sometimes I dream about what lies in the caves behind those walls, and I always wake up sweating. I told you I didn't know what happened to her, that I could probably guess. Now you know why."

He grabbed a paddle and eased the boat up to the dock. "You want to know the real horror of it, Detective?" he asked as he stepped out onto the boards and tied up. "You might think it's all about what happened back then, but it ain't; it's about how many people knew what was goin' on, and how they all stayed quiet about it, even today."

He looked at Jack, then at the notebook, and nodded at it. "It contains everything I saw. Everything I heard. Everythin' I was paid to forget. Maybe you can do something with it. I should have given it to Charlie. Me? I'm too old for redemption. Oh, and you might want to talk to Ruby Mae Collins. She'd be about seventy now, I should think. She worked with Grimes at the Brass Register. And Grimes had a younger sister, Sarah. She was seventeen at the time. Nice kid, she was. So was her sister, damn their eyes."

"Anyone else?" Jack asked.

"Hmm," he said, then thought for a moment, and continued. "Frank Whitaker; he was a security guard up there. Hell, we all knew each other. I remember him bragging about a big bonus, and you could try Margaret Wheeler. She was old man Caldwell's secretary, though she was damn closed mouth when Charlie interviewed her. Wouldn't say a word."

Jack waited for a few moments longer, wondering what was to come next. But the old man looked at him, then said, "That's it, sonny. That's all I got. Best get out of here before someone sees you talking to me."

But Jack didn't move. Instead, he said, "I have one last question, Sergeant. How many? How many are there buried up there in Forrest's Cave?"

Cooper was silent for a moment, replied, "I'm not rightly sure..." He shrugged, then said, with a straight face, "I was never there. They had a special team for what they called... underground storage. Forty... Fifty... Maybe more."

Jack opened his mouth to speak, but couldn't seem to find the words. He stood up. The boat rocked violently, threatening to tip him into the water. He waited until it steadied, then, very carefully, clambered up onto the dock, stood up, turned around and said, "Thank you for taking the time to talk to me, Mr. Cooper, and for your candor. It was... enlightening."

Cooper nodded without looking at him, but as Jack turned to leave, he said, "Detective? When this breaks—when it all comes out—remember this. Evil isn't just the man giving orders. Sometimes it's the man in the corner, staying quiet, taking his envelopes. Sometimes it's someone like me."

14

Monday afternoon

I WAS GETTING ready to leave for the day when there was a knock on my door. It opened and Jack stuck his head in and said, "You have a minute, Cap?"

I looked at my watch. It was almost four-thirty. I nodded, and he came in and sat down. He looked rough.

"Tough day?' I said. "You look like hell."

"Yeah… Well, you know," he said. "But you told me to check in, so here I am. I've just been out on Harrison Bay in a rickety old boat with Sergeant Cooper, and as it was… It was quite an experience, let me tell you. I did learn some stuff, though. I recorded everything. I'll make you a copy."

"Okay," I replied. "I thought we decided you'd drop by in the mornings."

He nodded. I could tell something was bothering him.

"What is it, Jack? What's bothering you?"

"This," he said. "It was almost the last thing he said to me."

He turned on the recorder and hit play.

"I have one last question, Sergeant," Jack said. "How many? How many are there buried up there in Forrest's cave?"

For a long moment, I heard nothing, then Cooper replied, "I'm not rightly sure..." another pause, then, "I was never there. They had a special team for... underground storage. Forty... Fifty... Maybe more."

He stopped the recording and looked at me, a weird look on his face, and I have to admit, I was stunned by what I'd heard.

"He also gave me this," he said and handed me an aging notebook. "I haven't had time to go through it in detail," he continued. "I just flipped through it. It's all there. He was quite meticulous, and he was very, very careful. It names names and tells quite a story, but there's nothing there we can use. From what I can tell, Cooper was just an observer, paid to keep his mouth shut.

"I talked to the chief," I said, flipping through the first few pages. "He said for you to go ahead and see where it takes us. I'm not sure what he meant by that, but it is what it is. So, the Grimes case is yours, if you want it. If it does involve the Caldwells, you have a problem, a big one." I snapped the book shut and handed it back to him."

"So that's it?" he said. "No help, just me?"

I nodded. "Yep. Look, Jack. It's just another old case. Unfortunately, it's gotten the attention of the media. It will sell some advertising. But we, and in this case that means me, don't have the resources for a full-blown investigation. If you want out, say so, and I'll assign it to someone else."

He slowly shook his head, looked at me for a moment, obviously considering his options, then said, "No, I'll do it. It's about time I had a case of my own."

"What about this?" he asked, holding up Cooper's notebook.

"Use what you can, ignore what you can't," I replied. "The last entry is dated June 1984." I shook my head. "It's useful, but I doubt any of it would be admissible. It's barely more than a code book. Cooper was careful how he wrote those notes. You have to read between the lines to make any sense of it. A good lawyer would tear it apart. The entries are ambiguous at best."

I knew I was disheartening him, but he needed to know what he was dealing with.

He sat silently for a moment, staring at me.

"So what you're telling me is that the sixty-one people who disappeared don't matter," he said. "Except for the one that caused a stir when her bones were recovered and the press got hold of it. That sucks, Kate."

"That's not what I said at all," I replied, not surprised by his outburst. "Of course they matter. What I'm saying is, go with the one you have. Solve that one and you'll likely solve the rest. From what I've heard, you'll be working with one of the foremost geological experts in the country. Dr. Croft knows more about caves and caving than anyone. The notebook…" I nodded at it, "will be helpful, as will your interviews with the long-retired witnesses, but the entries are all circumstantial. They could mean exactly what most people would think they mean: underground storage, permanent solution. Think about it" I shook my head. "The Caldwells—that is if that's who's behind these missing persons cases—were, as Cooper said, careful what they said and how they said it."

He nodded, obviously discouraged.

"So," I said. "How do you intend to proceed? What's your next step?"

He brightened visibly, smiled at me and said, "Dr. Croft. I need to get together with her. See what's she's found, if anything. And compare notes. And I still have several witnesses to interview. Cooper gave me some names. Grimes had a younger sister, and Charlie, my grandfather, interviewed Edwin Caldwell's secretary. He didn't get much out of her, apparently, but time and tide, right? Maybe she has a conscience. Maybe I can do better."

He stood up. "Thanks for listening, Kate, and for your insight. I'll keep you appraised."

"You're welcome, and please do," I said as he walked to the door.

I watched as he closed the door, and I couldn't help but sit and stare at it, thinking about what I hadn't said to him.

I had no doubt that what he was about to do was going to create a shitstorm among some of the movers and shakers of city and county, and I was wondering if he could handle it.

15

Monday Evening

JACK & AMELIA
   7:30pm

IT WAS five-thirty when Jack left Kate's office that Monday afternoon. He arrived home some twenty minutes later and, after cracking a beer, he called Amelia.

"Jack," she said when she picked up. "I was just thinking about you."

"Oh were you, now? Problems?"

"No," she replied. "I was just thinking; it's been five days. We should probably get together."

"Yeah, sorry. My fault. I've been kinda busy conducting interviews."

"And from that... good news or bad?" she asked.

"Good question," he replied. "A bit of both, I guess. The good news is, we have an ID. The bones are those of Mary Ellen Grimes. She went missing on April 15, 1974. The bad news; I've gathered a lot of information, most of it informative but useless. It's all old and mostly circumstantial and the statute of limitations has run out on almost all of it. Still, I should probably bring you up to speed with what I learned. How about you? Anything good."

"Depends on what you call good. Umm... have you eaten yet? We could talk over dinner."

He thought for a minute before hesitantly saying, "Sure. Where? What time?"

"Say an hour, at the country club? It's quiet there and we can talk privately."

The country club? Geez, he thought.

"Umm, I'm not a member."

"Not a problem," she replied. "I am. I'll leave word at the front desk. Dinner's on me."

"Well... Okay then. Fine. Say..." he looked at his watch, "seven-thirty?"

"Seven-thirty it is," she replied and ended the call.

Geez, what the hell am I going to wear? Damn, I sound like a frickin' woman.

He settled for tan pants, a white shirt, red tie and a navy suit jacket with his Glock discreetly holstered on his right hip beneath the jacket. *That, Jack North, will have to do,* he thought, then turned away from the mirror, grabbed his wallet and the notebook and walked out of the apartment. Twenty minutes later, he turned into the club driveway and into the parking lot. He parked in one of the visitor's slots, turned off the engine, and then sat there for several moments, thinking,

Finally, he took a deep breath and muttered, "Let's do this." And he got out of the car and walked up the steps and into the lobby where a young woman dressed in a black business suit approached him and said, "Detective North?"

He nodded.

She smiled at him and said, "Welcome to the Golf and

Country Club. If you'll follow me, please." And she led him to a table at the far end of the dining room, within fifteen feet of the bar, where Amelia was seated at a table by a window that overlooked the first tee.

"Jack," she said, rising to her feet. "How nice to see you again."

The young lady, still smiling, turned away, walked to the bar, said something to the bartender, then walked swiftly away.

He reached across the table and shook her hand, then he looked around the room. It was... not vast, but pretty big, and, because it was a Monday evening, so he thought, quiet. There were two couples and three small groups. All were casually dressed.

Amelia was wearing a simple black dress with a white wool shawl.

"It's nice to see you, too, Amelia," he replied, feeling more than a little self-conscious.

"I chose this table," she said as she sat down again, "because it's quiet and we can talk." She nodded to the hovering waiter.

"Let's eat first," she said. "I've had nothing since this morning. I'm starving."

Jack smiled.

"I'm going to have the crab cakes with mashed potato and broccoli," she said. "What would you like?"

He glanced at the menu, then looked up and said, "Sounds good to me. I'll have the same, thank you."

The waiter wrote it down, then looked at him and said, "And what would you like to drink, sir?"

"I'll have a beer, I think. D'you have Blue Moon?"

"Of course, sir. Bottle or draft?"

"Draft. Thank you."

They made small talk until their food arrived and then, for the most part, they ate in silence.

Jack, impatient to get to the point of the meeting, watched as the waiter cleared the table, then said, "So, anything to report?"

"Quite a bit, actually. What about you?"

"I've been conducting interviews. I told you the ME ID'd the remains, right?"

She nodded. "Yes, Doctor Sheddon also called me. Mary Ellen Grimes. Have you notified the relatives?"

"My boss has... I think. Geez, I'd better check to make sure. I'll do it in the morning. So, what d'you have?"

"You first," she said, smiling.

She was, he could tell, still a little wary and on the defensive. So he dove right in.

"I've talked to Chief Hargrove. That was interesting. He is, so it seems, full of regrets and suffering from a guilty conscience... And I interviewed Detective Morton, Officer Henderson and Sergeant Cooper. That one was the last, and the most interesting and productive, because he, too, wanted to unload. He gave me this."

He handed her the notebook Cooper had given him.

"But that wasn't all. Hargrove put me onto his secretary— she's living in Fort Walton Beach now—and she gave me a USB drive with all his records on it, records that should have been purged from the police database back in the 1980s. It's all good stuff, but little of it is actionable. The book," he nodded at it, "Cooper was very careful about what was entered and how into his notes, and Hargroves' records... Kate... I mean Captain Gazzara, reckons they're useful only for the information they contain. The statute of limitations has run out on everything but murder."

He paused for a moment and watched as she flipped through the pages of the notebook.

"I mean, look at this entry dated March 15, 1974," he said, taking it from her. He flipped through the pages until he found the one he was looking for.

"See?" he said, turning the book so she could see the entry.

Busy meeting. Preston brought maps of cave system. New areas marked in red. EC very interested in western tunnel network - 'perfect for storage.' Chief H looked uncomfortable. Later heard him in bathroom being sick.

"That's the day Mary Grimes went missing," Jack said. "And there's more. Look at this one."

He flipped through a couple more pages, then laid the book down in front of her.

April 18, 1974

Can't sleep. Keep seeing that girl's photo in paper. Family looking everywhere but the caves. God help me, I know and say nothing. Money feels heavier every month.

"And this one," he said, turning the pages.

May 1, 1974

Richard different from EC. More calculating. EC kills when necessary. Richard seems to enjoy it. God help us when he takes over.

"And then there are the tunnels," Jack said. "Cooper told me there were at least two connecting the cave system to the Mountain City Club, and that right after Grimes disappeared they began renovations, pouring concrete. What d'you make of that?"

"I know about the tunnels," she replied. "And I can show you, but we need to go to the university, to the library. You up for it?"

"What… now?" He furrowed his brow.

"Of course now. Unless you have something more important to do."

"Well, no, but—"

"Good," she said, cutting him off as she waved to get the waiter's attention.

She signed the bill, then said, "Come on. Let's go. You follow me, okay?"

The UTC library's Special Collections department was a vast and rather dusty room wherein were collections of papers, documents, maps and books—stacked on tall shelves separated by oversized oak tables—some of which dated back to the university's founding. It was, in fact, quite a famous research facility. Amelia obviously knew her way around the library and had obviously been working there for at least a couple of days, because there were geological surveys and maps spread across three tables.

"Really?" Jack asked as he stood at her side and stared at it all.

She smiled. "A bit overwhelming, isn't it? But not really. Not when you know what you're doing. Look here; the 1958 Tennessee Cave Survey shows three main passages in Forrest's Cave. But here, by 1962, the western passage has vanished from the records, though there's a footnote here that mentions 'extensive limestone dissolution features.' And this one, the 1967 survey might as well be mapping a different cave system entirely." She'd marked the discrepancies with red sticky notes, creating a constellation of inconsistencies.

Jack looked around. The room smelled of dust and forgotten things.

"I've digitized most of it," she said, "but I thought it would be easier for me to show it all to you... like this, spread out so you can see it."

"Gee, thanks," Jack muttered.

She laughed.

"Look at this one," she said, leaning over the table. "It's a 1957 survey. I almost missed it. It was misfiled."

It looked older. Its edges were crumbling. "There was something about it," she said. "Something I couldn't make sense of, at least not at first. These are not standard geological markings. It's the same cave system, but the layout differs subtly from all the other surveys, and it shows an entrance that appears in no other documentation. And look at the margins. These handwritten notes: they're detailed calculations for blast patterns and support structures. The notes are technical, precise, and made by someone planning major modifications to the natural cave system. I mean, look at them. What do they tell you?"

Limestone stability critical at junction points.

Additional reinforcement required for weight-bearing loads.

Blast sequence must maintain natural appearance.

He stared at them, but didn't answer.

"And look at the stamp," she said. "'County Resolution 47-B: Approved for Mining Operations.' The resolution number doesn't follow standard formatting for the period. I don't get it. Someone's been up to something, and I want to know what."

"But what does any of this have to do with Mary Ellen's murder?" Jack asked.

"I don't know, yet," she replied. "But something. I'm sure of it. And then there's this. If it's not a smoking gun, I don't know what is."

She pointed to the bottom corner where he could see, almost hidden by a coffee stain, a cryptic note, a set of initials, and a date: 'Reroute approved - J.F.H. March 1964.'

"Those are Judge Franklin Harrison's initials," she said, "the same judge who signed off on multiple expedited property transfers to the Caldwell Mining Company."

Amelia pulled up her timeline database on her iPad. "Here's where it all connects with our investigation."

He smiled at the use of the word 'our.'

"March 14, 1974," she continued. "That's one month before Mary Ellen Grimes disappeared, and the beginning of the spike in missing persons cases. The coordinates place this hidden entrance on private Caldwell property, away from the tourist areas and regular mining operations.

"I searched all the records," she continued, "even the old card catalogs and judicial records. County Resolution 47-B doesn't exist in any official capacity. But the blueprint tells us it should.

Someone has gone to a great deal of trouble to create an entrance that technically never existed, and approved by paperwork that never officially existed, and just before people started disappearing. Jack, this isn't just evidence of geological manipulation, it's proof of premeditation. That, if I'm right, means capital murder. Someone carefully planned and constructed a secret entrance to the cave system, complete with official-looking documentation to deflect casual investigation. And they did it just before the killing started. What d'you think?"

Jack almost laughed. "You're serious, aren't you?" He asked.

She looked stunned. "Yes, damn it. I'm serious. Why wouldn't I be? It's all there, in the records. All we have to do is prove it. And that's what I want to do. How about you? Are you serious? How many more bodies are there up there in those caves, d'you think?"

"According to Sergeant Cooper, maybe fifty. Maybe more," he muttered, staring down at the maps. "I found sixty-one missing person reports for the period." He shrugged. "Yes... I'm serious."

"You want to meet up for breakfast in the morning, then, before we go underground?"

Underground? Jack shuddered at the thought. It wasn't that he was claustrophobic, which he was, at least a little; it was more a deep-seated fear of the unknown, and his lack of control over it.

"Underground, huh?" he said. "Well, yeah, okay, I guess. Sounds like a plan. When and where?"

"Hardees do the best biscuits, so..." she looked at him, her eyebrows raised in question.

He nodded. "The one on Broad, at eight? Or would you like me to pick you up... somewhere?"

She smiled and shook her head. "There's no need for that. Hardees on Broad at eight will be fine. Oh, and wear something old and tough. D'you have some good boots? If so, wear them. I'll bring the rest of what we need. In the meantime, I'll call you if something comes up. Let's get out of here, shall we?"

"Good... Yeah. Call me. You going to leave all this out? Shouldn't we put it away? It's important stuff, right?"

"No, it will be fine. We respect one another around here."

"Well, if you say so," he said, and followed her to the elevator and then to the ground floor exit.

"Have a good night, Jack," she said as she went to her car. "See you tomorrow morning."

He grunted something she didn't catch, so she shook her head, got into her car and drove away.

CHAPTER 16,

Tuesday Morning

The Cave
    Jack
    8am

Amelia arrived promptly at eight. They enjoyed a quick breakfast of sausage and egg biscuits and coffee, and then Jack followed her out to her car.

"See you at the cave?" she said. "Follow me and stay close. I want to take a look at that unmapped entrance first."

Thirty minutes later, they were standing before the concrete seal blocking the unmapped entrance. She stared at it for a moment then looked at him and shook her head. "The engineering's professional grade, Jack," she said.

He nodded. "You'd know that better than me," he admitted.

"This seal was installed decades ago," she said. "See how the concrete's weathered?" She shook her head again, then sighed and said, "There's nothing we can do here. Let's go see what we can find underground."

"Yeah, right," he said, though his reply lacked enthusiasm. "You lead the way."

The uniformed cop in a police cruiser rolled down his window. Jack flashed him his badge, and he waved them through. It was fifteen after nine, so he figured he'd better check in with Marcus Webb, the site manager.

He pulled up outside the site office, got out and waved for Amelia to join him, then mounted the two steps, knocked once, and opened the door. Webb was seated at his desk doing something on his computer, but he clicked his mouse and closed it down when he saw Jack.

"Detective," he said. "Good morning. I hope this visit means you're going to let me get back to work."

"Sorry," Jack replied with a wry smile as Amelia joined him. "It's going to be a while, I'm afraid. We think there may be more bodies buried down there, so we're going to go in and take a look. We're just checking in as a courtesy. Is there anything we should know before we proceed?"

Webb heaved a sigh, pursed his lips and shook his head. "Other than I had a visit from the owners, no," he replied. "Needless to say, they're not happy. D'you have any idea how much longer it's going to take?"

Jack shook his head. "There's no telling until we do a thorough search of the cave system." He looked at Amelia.

"Several days, at least," she said, "and then it will depend on what we find."

Webb sighed again and shook his head. "I'll let the owners know. Might as well shut things down completely then until you're done. Geez, this is costing us a fortune. Oh well, it can't be helped, I suppose." Again, he shook his head, obviously exasperated.

"What's your plan, then?" He asked.

Jack looked at Amelia.

"We're going to do a preliminary inspection," she said. "Then I need to… We need to make a full and complete survey. If there are indeed more bodies, we need to find them."

"That's quite a project," Webb replied. "There are miles of caves and mining tunnels. Most of them shut down, blocked off. What you're suggesting could take months. And you're going with her?" He looked at Jack. "Just the two of you?"

"For now, yes," Jack replied.

"And you've caving experience?" Webb persisted.

"Well… no," Jack replied, "but…"

He looked at Amelia.

"He'll be fine," she said, "so long as he does as he's told." She smiled.

Jack frowned.

"You ready?" she asked.

Jack nodded.

Webb grinned. "Good luck," he said. "I'm glad it's you and not me."

Jack parked his car beside the site office and rode with Amelia to the cave entrance, which was crisscrossed with yellow crime scene tape.

"You ready?" she asked as she exited the car, went around the back and opened up the rear hatch to reveal the cargo space loaded with caving gear, including helmets with mounted headlamps, protective oversuits, knee pads, elbow pads, and gloves.

"Here," she said, "put these on," as she handed him an oversuit. "And these and this."

"You're looking good," she said, smiling at his obvious discomfort. Jack was by then wearing the suit, knee and elbow pads, and a bright yellow helmet with a double headlamp attached and a backup lamp attached to his belt, along with a pair of gloves and, for some reason he couldn't have explained, his Glock in its holster on his belt under the suit.

His discomfort increased. "I feel like a damn turtle," he said.

"You'll get over it," she said. "It will be cold and damp down there. The suit will keep you warm, perhaps uncomfortably warm, but it will protect you. Now, some rules. First and most important, we stay together. You do not, under any circumstances, go off on your own. Understood?"

"Yes, of course," he replied.

"Second, we do as little damage to the environment as possible."

"Got it," he replied.

"Third, you do exactly as I say, without question. It's important. Our safety depends on it."

"I get it," he replied, tugging at the stiff suit collar.

"Good. Let's go. Try to keep up."

And Jack followed her under the tape and into the cave toward the crime scene lights shining dimly in the distance.

Jack shuddered as Amelia marched on toward the lights where she stopped only for a moment to ensure that nothing had been disturbed, then she turned to him and said, "From here on we're going into territory that hasn't been explored in over fifty years, at least that's what the reports say. So stay close. Gloves on?"

She looked at him. He held up his gloved hands for her to see.

"Good," she said as she adjusted her helmet's chin strap and double-checked the backup light clipped to her harness.

Involuntarily, Jack mimicked her, and then followed her into the darkness, his headlamp casting stark shadows on the rocky walls. He was already feeling constrained in the narrow confines of Forrest's Cave's lesser-known passages.

Amelia said little as she pushed onward, pausing periodically to consult her compass and the detailed geological survey maps she carried stored in a waterproof case. The cave temperature was a constant fifty-five degrees, but the humidity was making it feel warmer than it actually was, causing sweat to bead on their foreheads.

The sound of water was omnipresent. Not just the steady drip-drip-drip, but also the distant murmur of an underground stream somewhere in the cave system's lower levels. The acoustic properties of the limestone chambers created odd echoes, making it difficult to pinpoint the source of the sound. Jack was both fascinated, edgy and claustrophobic as they moved onward, and the cave walls seemed to close in around them. Their head-lamps illuminated countless speleothems, stalactites, stalagmites, curtains of flowstone that had formed over millennia, casting shadows that moved and undulated as they forged onward.

Amelia moved slowly forward, her trained eye spotting details others might miss: unusual wear patterns on rock faces, inconsistent with natural water erosion. In one narrow corridor, she spotted tool marks partially obscured by newer mineral deposits —clear evidence of human modification that shouldn't exist in this supposedly untouched section of the cave. She documented her findings with her camera, the flash momentarily flooding the passage with harsh light.

The passage suddenly narrowed significantly, transforming into what cavers call a "squeeze," a tight tunnel that required them to crawl on their bellies. Jack hesitated for a moment. His breathing quickened. Sweat dripped from the tip of his nose despite the cool air, and his hands shook slightly as he adjusted his gear, then dropped to his knees and followed Amelia into the squeeze. On his belly, now, the confined space triggered something in his mind he'd never before experienced, a deep-seated, primordial fear. He bit his lip, forcing himself onward, close to panic. The rough rock seemed to press in from all sides as they inched forward on their elbows and knees.

Fortunately for Jack, the squeeze was a short one, less than a hundred feet, that opened suddenly into a large chamber, their lights revealing a space roughly fifty feet in diameter with a ceiling high enough to stand erect.

"You okay," she asked, her voice echoing hollowly around the chamber. She sounded concerned.

"Whew!" He blew air out through his lips. "That was... something else," he said, the beam of his headlamp bouncing off the walls as he looked around. "Hey, what's that?" he asked, pointing at something white close against the dark rock wall.

Amelia looked where he was pointing, then said, "That looks like..." she stepped closer. "It's a human skull," she said as she knelt down. "It's partially embedded in flowstone."

She stood up without touching it and looked around the chamber.

"There are more," she said. "Over there. Bones, and... What the hell?"

She stepped forward, bent over, her headlamp illuminating the ground in front of her.

"Stay where you are, Jack," she said as she crouched down again. "There are bones everywhere."

She rejoined Jack. "There's a Zippo lighter just over there. It has some initials on it. It's next to what looks like a delicate silver charm bracelet. And there's a pair of horn-rimmed glasses. It's partially buried and one of the lenses is cracked.

It was at that moment they heard a low rumble emanating from somewhere behind them, accompanied by the sound of stone grinding against stone. The air was filled with fine dust drifting down from above, catching the light of their headlamps, twinkling like miniature stars.

"That's not natural," she whispered, grabbing Jack's arm. "The resonance pattern... someone's using explosives. I think it's on the far side of the mountain, but the shock waves—"

There was another rumble, closer this time. Dust and small stones showered down from above.

"They're trying to seal us in," Jack yelled. "We need to get the hell out of here, now! We can't go back. I can't do it, Amelia. Not that way. What if it falls in on us? What if it's already closed?"

"Stop it, Jack," she snapped. "There's no need to panic. There has to be another way out. They couldn't have gotten the bodies through that squeeze. But first, I need to document all this," and she began to photograph the remains. That quickly done, she took several soil samples, picked up the lighter and pocketed it, and then grabbed a section of jawbone and pocketed that.

Barely had she finished when there was another rumble, much louder this time, and rock dust billowed out of the tunnel behind them.

"It's gone," Jack yelled. "The tunnel's collapsed. We're trapped!"

CHAPTER 17

Tuesday Afternoon

THE CAVE

   Jack

   5pm

"THEY'RE TRYING to seal us in," Jack shouted. "We need to move. Now."

Amelia grabbed Jack's arm. "This way," she snapped. And together, they ran across the rocky floor to the far side of the chamber, where they found a narrow tunnel carved out of the rock.

"This way," Amelia shouted and ran into the tunnel.

Jack followed her, but barely were they a dozen feet in, when Jack's newfound claustrophobia really kicked in. He was in a cold sweat. His heart was racing. His hands were shaking. The walls seemed to press closer, and he stopped, barely able to breathe.

"Amelia," he croaked.

She stopped, turned, backed up, held out her hand and said,

"Hold my hand. Focus on my light. We're in a maintenance tunnel. See the markers on the wall? They were installed back in the sixties by the miners. OSHA requirements. Count them with me. They're spaced exactly thirty feet apart."

Another explosion rocked the cave and the maintenance tunnel groaned under the stress of shifting rock.

Hand in hand, Jack following Amelia, they navigated the tunnel until they reached a vertical shaft with metal rungs embedded in the rock wall. Amelia tilted her head back to shine her light up the shaft.

"There's an exit hatch up there," she shouted. "Are you able to climb?"

Jack nodded violently, his breath coming in short gasps. And they began to climb. Twenty feet up, one of the rungs gave way under Jack's boot and he almost fell. Hanging on for dear life, he paused, took a deep breath, then slowly, gently, he climbed onward and upward until finally; they reached the hatch, just as the biggest blast yet hit. Jack threw his weight against the metal door as Amelia frantically worked the emergency release. With a shriek of protesting metal, the door opened to the early evening air.

Amelia rolled out onto the rain-slick limestone. Seconds later, Jack followed her, and they lay there on their backs, gasping for air.

Jack sat up and looked around. They were higher up the mountain than he expected. A steep slope led down to where the lights at the main cave entrance glowed in the gathering dusk. Through gaps in the trees, they could see the tourist parking lot about four hundred yards away to the south, their own vehicles, Jack's to the left of the site office and Amelia's a lonely silhouette under the security lights.

"Geez, Amelia," he said, "we've been down there for over eight hours."

"Time flies when you're having fun," Amelia said with a wry smile.

"That shed over there," she said, recognizing the rusted building. "It's a mining company maintenance building, I think. It's not on the tourist maps, and it probably hasn't been used since they updated the main entrance back in the '90s."

Jack scanning the thick undergrowth, noting the recent tire tracks cutting through the moss and fallen leaves. "Someone's been up here, despite the 'No Access' signs marking this as private Caldwell property. Can you get some photos of these tracks?"

Amelia scrambled to her feet, took her camera from a utility pocket, and snapped several closeup images of the tracks.

"Look at this," Amelia called softly, examining the hatch from which they'd just emerged. "I bet it was installed more than sixty years ago. We should never have been able to open it," she said, "But look, the hinges have been oiled recently. Someone's maintaining this exit. But why?"

"Yeah," Jack said, breathing easier now they were out in the open. "And by whom? That's the question."

From their elevated position, they had a clear view of the cave operations below. "It's the perfect spot for surveillance," Jack said, looking around. "You could watch everything from up here, the main entrance, the service roads, everything, without being seen."

Amelia checked her GPS, then her map. "We're about eighty feet above, and some four hundred yards to the northeast of the main cave entrance. This entire area is Caldwell Mining property. It's separated from the tourist lease." She gestured to the old shed. "That building doesn't show up on any recent surveys. Officially, this access point doesn't exist."

The rumble of another collapse echoed up from below. "I think someone just sealed off the trail to the remains we discovered," Jack said. "We need to move. Whoever set those charges will be checking to make sure they worked."

"Good thing I have photos, then," she said grimly.

"Yeah, that," Jack said. "Come on." He took her arm and helped her over the tough terrain as they made their way carefully down the slope, using the trees for cover.

"The old service road would have been quicker," she muttered as they stumbled along, "but it's also more exposed..." She stopped talking for a moment, then said, "It's also exactly what you'd want for moving things, or people, in and out of the cave system unobserved."

"Yeah, and someone knew we were down there," Jack said. "We have a leak somewhere."

"And they have expert knowledge of the cave system's weak points," Amelia added. "Those explosions were precisely placed."

They made it back to their vehicles just as darkness was falling. "You know the discovery of those remains has escalated the investigation beyond any chance of turning back?" Jack said.

She nodded, a hand on his arm to steady herself.

They stumbled out onto the parking lot close to the cave entrance and Jack stopped, turned around, and looked back up the mountain. The shed and the emergency hatch had blended back into the undergrowth, invisible unless you knew where to look.

"What now?" Amelia asked as she opened her car door.

Jack looked at his watch. It was just after 6pm. "I need to call this in. We have a major incident here and I don't know how to handle it. And, I don't know about you, but I need something to eat—"

"Yes, well, so do I," she said, cutting him off.

"Let me make the call and then we'll see," he said.

CHAPTER 18

Monday Evening

KATE

6:30pm

I WAS ABOUT to leave for the day when my cell phone rang and somehow I just knew it was Jack and that things on the mountain were about to escalate.

Not wanting to use the radio, he'd called me on his cell and was pretty wound up.

"Captain?" he snapped. "We have a situation at Forrest's Cave. I need you out here ASAP."

Thirty minutes later, I pulled into the empty tourist parking off to the west of the main entrance to Forrest's Cave. Jack and Amelia were waiting for me at the edge of the lot, Jack looking like he'd lost a dollar and found a dime, both of them filthy, covered in muck.

Amelia was sitting on a low stone wall, her fingers moving rapidly over her iPad.

"Talk to me, Jack," I said, "and it had better be good."

"Captain, we found at least three sets of skeletal remains in an unmapped section of the cave," he began, obviously trying to keep himself in check despite the adrenaline still pumping through his system. "One female based on bone structure, so Amelia said." He turned to look at her. "At least forty years old, judging by the calcification. We also found personal effects— jewelry, glasses. Unfortunately, we were unable to collect any of it, but she photographed and documented everything. Kate, they tried to kill us. They tried to bury us in there. I'm not kidding. They used dynamite to blow up the tunnels. We barely made it out."

I stared at him. I'd said it better be good. This was way more than I expected.

"You're sure they used explosives?" I asked. It was a stupid question, but I didn't know what else to say, not at that point, anyway.

He looked at me as if I was an idiot. "Yeah!" he said sarcastically.

I looked at Croft. She was working hard, uploading what she had to her encrypted cloud storage.

I stepped over to her. "Can I take a look, please, Amelia?" I asked.

She looked up at me, her eyes wide. She hesitated for a second, then nodded and handed me the tablet.

"Flip from left to right," she said.

The images told their own story: bones partially embedded in limestone, a delicate charm bracelet that had somehow survived decades in the cave's depths, distinctive tool marks on the cave walls that suggested the bodies had been deliberately placed.

"And there's this," she said and handed me a Zippo lighter. Then she looked at Jack, who was now at my side. "All the images are backed up to three secure servers," she said. "One at the university, one off-site, and one even the Caldwells can't reach."

She held up her hand for the tablet. I handed it back to her and she pulled up the GPS coordinates of their location when they made the discovery and added them to her geological survey map.

"There's more, Captain," Jack said, watching Amelia work. "We found evidence of recent activity; fresh tool marks, modern climbing gear. Someone's been accessing that section of the cave, and they didn't want us finding it. They used some serious explosives to try to seal us in. Precisely placed charges, not some amateur job."

Amelia glanced at the cave entrance. "And Captain—based on the blast patterns—whoever did this knows the caves well. This isn't just an old body dump site; it's an active operation."

"Go on," I said.

"We went in through the main tourist entrance," Jack said, "following Dr. Croft's geological survey maps. About eight hundred feet in, we found a narrow passage that wasn't on any of her maps, and there were what looked to me like recent tool marks around the entrance."

He ran his hand through his dust-covered hair. "The passage led to a chamber roughly fifty feet in diameter, Amelia's estimate," he said, looking at her. "That's where we found the remains. Like I said, the first one, a female, was partially embedded in the limestone wall. Amelia reckons they've been there at least forty years based on the… calcification patterns."

"The others?" I asked.

"Scattered across the chamber floor," he replied. "Two more sets of remains that we could see clearly, maybe more buried in the sediment, and the personal effects. That monogrammed lighter, a charm bracelet, a pair of horn-rimmed glasses. All consistent with the 1960s time period… So she said."

He gestured toward the cave entrance. "We were documenting the scene when we felt the first tremor. Amelia knew it wasn't natural. She figured someone was using explosives to seal off the chamber. Kate, whoever it was, they knew exactly where to place those charges. We barely made it out."

"How *did* you get out?" I asked.

"Through a maintenance tunnel and up a shaft to an old emergency exit. Amelia figured it was pretty old. We barely made it up the shaft before the main passage collapsed." He paused, turned around, and pointed to a spot high on the mountain. "There," he said. "The exit is hidden in that clump of trees."

He turned back to me, looked me in the eye and said, "Someone wants those remains to stay buried, and they were willing to kill us to make it happen."

"And you think this is connected to the Grimes' disappearance?" I asked.

He shrugged. "Has to be. The timeline fits. And, Kate? That chamber also showed signs of regular use. Whatever we stumbled into down there, it's not just about old bodies. Something's still going on in those caves."

Inwardly, I shook my head. "Give me a minute," I said and turned and walked slowly away, thinking, mentally shifting the pieces into place. It wasn't looking good. And, after more than two decades on the force, I could recognize when a case is about to explode. This one had all the signs.

"Here's how we play it," I said, returning to Jack. "I'm calling in the state police and the FBI. This crosses jurisdictions, missing persons, more possible homicides, the attempted murder of a police officer, criminal use of explosives. The more agencies involved, the harder it'll be for anyone to bury this."

He nodded, and I took out my phone and called Chief Johnston. "Chief," I said when he answered, "I need the state police at Forrest's Cave, and Mike Willis and his full team... No, it's too compli— Yes, Chief, now... No, this can't wait till morning... Yes... Of course... The FBI? That's my next call. Yes, sir. I'll keep you... Yes... Yes... Of course—" And then he hung up on me.

Why am I not surprised? I thought as I punched in the number for the FBI field office... "This is Captain Catherine Gazzara, Chattanooga PD. I need to speak with SAIC Thompson, please... Yes, I'll hold."

I knew Thompson quite well, so it was a quick conversation during which he agreed to send a full team to process the cave.

That done, I turned again to Jack, I said: "Document everything. I want a full report before you leave tonight. And Jack? Leave nothing out. Every detail, no matter how small. Once the Caldwells hear about this, things are going to move fast."

I turned to Amelia. "Dr. Croft, I'm going to need all your geological data. Photographs, surveys, everything you've documented. Can you get me a preliminary report on the age of those remains?"

"Yes, of course," she replied.

My calls set off a chain reaction. Within an hour, the tourist parking lot had been transformed into a sea of emergency vehicles. Red and blue lights painted the limestone cliff face in alternating colors as the state police established a perimeter, pushing back gathering onlookers and local news crews drawn by their scanners.

I waited until the emergency vehicles began to arrive, then I called my friend, Assistant District Attorney Larry Strange. "Larry? It's Kate Gazzara. Remember that conversation we had about the Caldwell family? Yeah. I think we just found what you were looking for."

To the gathering group of officers and agents, I began to lay out the plan. First, I had my uniformed officers secure the scene. Then I instructed Mike to get his team in there as soon as Webb's structural engineers had cleared the way through the collapsed section of tunnel. Ten minutes later, well, maybe twenty, after a preliminary inspection, I was told it was going to take days to clear the tunnel. *Why am I not surprised?* I thought.

Finally, I called my partner, Sergeant Corbin Russell, and had him gather the rest of my team and had him pull every missing persons case from the 1960s forward and start background checks on everyone with access to the cave system. I also had him organize protection details for both Jack and Amelia.

"And one more thing, Corbin," I added. "Everything goes through my office. No exceptions. Someone's been covering up murders in this town for decades. That stops today."

Jack and Amelia were standing near her vehicle, both still covered in cave dust, as she completed her final transfer. Me? I was a few yards away talking to Corbin on the phone, but I heard her say, "The timeline's crucial here. The calcification patterns on the remains, the tool marks; everything has to be documented before someone tries to muddy or destroy the evidence."

The first FBI arrived in force a few moments later. Three black SUVs pulled in one after the other with practiced precision and reversed almost to the cliff face where they parked.

For several moments, nothing happened, and I couldn't see from where I was standing, but then the doors opened almost as one, and Special Agent Regis Thompson emerged from the lead vehicle. He was a tall, slightly-built man whose long, casual stride belied his focused expression. I knew from previous cases, as did Jack, that he was a straight shooter, honest, but ambitious.

"Kate, North," Thompson nodded as he approached. "Want to tell me why I'm looking at a joint task force operation on a Monday night?"

But before I could answer, more vehicles arrived: the state police and a Mobile Command Center. And... the night air was filled with the radio chatter and the slamming of car doors as three different agencies began setting up their stations.

"...three sets of remains, possibly more," Jack said, briefing Thompson. "Dating back to the '60s. That's based on Dr. Croft's preliminary analysis. And someone just tried to seal us in there with explosives."

Thompson's eyebrows rose. "Seriously?" he asked.

"Less than two hours ago," Jack replied. "Someone knew what

they were doing, that's for sure. Someone who knows these caves."

My phone rang. It was a blocked number. I smiled and answered it. I had a good idea what it would be about, and I was right.

I stepped over to where Jack was still talking to Thompson and said, "I just got word. The Caldwells are on their way. Their lawyers have drafted cease and desist orders based on property rights."

"Let them try," Thompson said. "Attempted murder of a police officer trumps property rights, right?"

I nodded, but said nothing.

More vehicles arrived, expensive ones, black SUVs with tinted windows parked at the edge of the chaos. Five men in suits emerged, followed by Edwin Caldwell himself. Despite his age, he moved with authority, his face a mask of concern.

"Captain Gazzara," he called out as he approached. "I just heard. A terrible business. Of course, our family will cooperate fully, but I'm concerned about the structural integrity of the cave system. I think we should seal the site until proper surveys—"

"Mr. Caldwell," I said, "I believe you know Agent Thompson from previous interactions. We'll need access to all your cave surveys and maintenance records."

Caldwell's mask slipped at the mention of records. The old man's eyes swiveled to the cave entrance, then back to me.

"Of course, of course. Our office will provide everything tomorrow—"

"Now," Thompson said. "We'll send a team with you to collect them. Tonight."

And then the arguments began. Questions of jurisdiction, chain of command, evidence processing protocols. It was always the same, a bureaucratic nightmare.

And then, everything changed.

Amelia approached, a concerned look on her face. She put a

hand on Jack's arm and said, "Jack, someone's accessing the cave system from another entrance. My seismic monitors are showing activity in the western tunnels."

He looked at the circus developing in the parking lot, then at me. I nodded. He looked back at her and said, "How fast can you get us there?"

"Ten minutes. I know a maintenance access point."

He looked again at me. Again, I nodded, a subtle signal my team knows well. "You have your weapon?" I muttered.

He nodded, and I told him to go, "But be careful," I said in a low voice. "We still don't know how high this goes."

CHAPTER 19

Monday Evening

THE CAVE

Jack

8pm

As JACK and Amelia slipped away from the chaos, he glanced back at Edwin Caldwell. The old man was watching them, his mask completely gone now. The look in his eyes made Jack's hand move instinctively to his weapon.

The game had changed. Jack knew that, but there was still work to do. For one, the cave had not yet given up all its secrets. And for two, somewhere in the darkness beneath Lookout Mountain, someone was very busy destroying evidence.

"Your vehicle or mine?" He asked.

She gave him one of those looks. He grinned at her, then nodded. Five minutes later, Amelia's SUV was lurching along an overgrown service road through Mitchell's pass—so named for the Union Cavalry General Robert B. Mitchell—to the western slopes of the mountain. Amelia's hands gripping the wheel, fighting to keep the vehicle on the track despite the rough terrain.

She's done this before, Jack thought, hanging onto the strap as the passenger side front wheel dipped into a deep rut, then out again, throwing him hard against the door.

"The western tunnel system was supposedly sealed in '65," she explained as she parked the vehicle behind an abandoned maintenance shed. "It was officially condemned after a major collapse that caused the death of three miners. But my monitoring equipment's been picking up regular activity." She took her iPad from her bag and pulled up a graph showing seismic readings. "See?" She pointed to a graph. "Like now."

Jack nodded, took his Glock from its holster, checked the weapon, then his backup piece. "How far to the entrance?"

"Maybe a quarter mile. There's an old mining access point hidden behind an old shed. Or there was. If they haven't destroyed it. Better suit up."

And they did, and a few minutes later were creeping along a narrow trail, through the darkness with their headlamps off, using only ambient moonlight to light the way.

The entrance was easy enough to find. It looked as though it had been abandoned long ago: the weathered boards nailed across a crumbling, timber-framed opening bore two faded 'DANGER' signs. But Jack's trained eyes took in the subtle signs of recent activity: recent tire tracks partially covered with scattered leaves, fresh tool marks on the boards.

"Someone's trying very hard to make this look like it's not been used in decades," he muttered.

Amelia nodded. "It's all an illusion," she said. "Look," she pointed, "that 'condemned' barrier is actually a door. It's been made to look like a barrier, but those hinges aren't that old and they've been painted over with rust-colored paint."

She nodded at the lock and chain hanging from the clasp. It

was unlocked and hanging loose. She grabbed the edge of the door with both hands and pulled. The door swung easily open.

They looked at each other. Amelia took a deep breath, nodded and stepped inside, into a well-maintained tunnel that sloped downward into the darkness.

"Modern support beams," Amelia whispered, playing her light across the ceiling. "The ventilation system's new, too. Someone's invested serious money here. It's in regular use… Listen. Can you hear it?"

"Sounds like a machine of some sort," he replied.

"Come on," Amelia said, and started down the tunnel.

"Wait," Jack said, putting a hand on her arm. "Better let me take the lead," Jack unholstered his weapon.

Slowly, carefully, they moved onward and downward, following the distant sounds of machinery.

The path was worn smooth, coated with the limestone dust, electrical cables running along the walls, security cameras hidden amongst old mining equipment. The beams of their flashlights casting stark shadows.

"Wait!" Jack stopped suddenly, holding up his hand. "Listen. Someone's down there."

The faint sound of voices echoed through the tunnel from somewhere up ahead; that and the sound of vehicles, heavy vehicles with their engines running.

"I don't like this," Jack said. "Maybe we should go back and call for help."

But Amelia pushed past him. Reluctantly, he followed.

The tunnel widened, then opened into a large chamber, brightly lit with industrial lighting.

"Geez, c'mere," Jack snapped as he grabbed her arm and pulled her behind a stack of wooden pallets.

The cavern in front and below was a hive of activity. Men in mining company coveralls were busily loading trucks. Two forklifts were moving heavy crates from one point to another while a third was loading them onto the trucks.

Jack frowned. Something's off about the scene.

"Those aren't mining company vehicles," he whispered. "They're not dump trucks. Look at the wheelbase. Those are custom, over-the-road long-haul transports."

"Jack." Amelia whispered. "Look at the crates. They're ventilated."

The implications of what they were seeing hit home just as a scream echoed from somewhere deeper in the tunnel system. It was quickly stifled, but still unmistakably human.

"We need to—" Jack began, but Amelia grabbed his arm.

"Shush," she whispered. "I can hear something behind us. I think someone's coming."

They both turned, their backs to the pallets, Jack's gun at the ready.

Back up the tunnel, they could see the wavering beams of flashlights. Jack looked around. *No escape route. No frickin' backup either*, he thought. And somewhere up ahead, someone's life was hanging in the balance.

Jack glanced at Amelia. Her eyes were mysterious pools of liquid in the darkness. "I guess we're about to find out what it is the Caldwells have been hiding in these caves," he whispered. "If we survive the next few minutes."

Jack grabbed her arm and pulled her behind a stack of empty crates. The sound of approaching footsteps, now from both directions, grew louder. His mind raced as he considered the options—none of them good. They were too deep in the tunnel system to make contact with the outside, and the noise of the trucks would drown out any calls for help.

"There should be a maintenance shaft about twenty feet over to the right," Amelia whispered in his ear. "If I'm right, it runs parallel to this tunnel. It will be a tight fit, I think, but—"

Another scream echoed through the cavern, followed by the sharp sound of a slap.

A man's voice shouted, "Shut her up!"

"Geez, that one was close," Jack said as, for the umpteenth time, he checked his phone; no signal. There was no way to alert Kate. Their only advantage was that no one knew they were there... yet.

The sound of footsteps grew closer. Jack counted at least three sets approaching from behind, and more from up ahead. From the shadows on the wall, he could see the approaching men were armed.

"The shaft," he whispered. "How far does it go?"

"It should connect to the main ventilation system. It should get us up above their operation."

They edged to the right, staying in the shadows. The maintenance shaft entrance was barely visible, a rusted grate set low in the wall. Jack covered their retreat while Amelia worked the grate loose. It took some doing but finally, with a loud scraping sound, she was able to pull it open.

Someone in the loading area shouted, "Get those crates loaded! Boss wants this place cleared before the feds start poking around upstairs. Come on. Hurry it up."

The grate came loose just as a beam of light swept over the stack of pallets they'd just vacated. Amelia slipped inside; Jack followed. Amelia was right. It was a tight squeeze. He pulled the grate shut behind him. Then, with his shoulders brushing both sides, and barely enough room to crouch-walk, he scrambled after her, feeling as if the world was closing in around him. He breathed hard, deeply, fighting off the panic that was threatening to overwhelm him.

They paused as boots passed directly above them. Through gaps in the grating, they could see several pairs of feet: combat boots, not mining footwear.

"Clear back here," a voice called out.

"Keep checking," someone replied. "Boss said two people slipped away from that circus up there. They could be anywhere."

Jack felt Amelia grab his hand and squeeze it. He squeezed back. "This isn't random," he said. "It's an organized search. They know we're here."

The shaft sloped gradually upward.

They moved on as quietly as possible; every sound seemingly amplified a thousand times in the confined space. He could hear water drip, his worst nightmare. The screams had stopped, but the echo of truck engines and voices continued below.

Amelia stopped suddenly, held up her hand, and pointed to a grate up ahead where the light from below seeped through. Together, they edged forward until they were over the grate and could peer down into what appeared to be a control center. He could see a bank of monitors showing security feeds. A half-dozen men in tactical gear were checking weapons. And, in the corner, strapped to a chair...

"I know her," Jack whispered. "That's Agent Thompson's partner, Agent Sarah Marshall. What the hell's she doing here? She's supposed to be on vacation."

"Look at her clothes," Amelia whispered. "She's been here a while, by the look of her. They must have known the investigation was coming."

"Yeah, but how?" Jack whispered. "Hey, look. See who that is?"

Below them, a familiar figure had entered the room. Richard Caldwell, impeccably dressed despite the filthy environment, approached the captured agent.

"Now then, Agent Marshall," his voice carried clearly up through the grating. "Let's discuss exactly what the FBI knows about our little operation."

Jack and Amelia watched helplessly through the grating as Caldwell slowly circled Agent Marshall's chair. Even tied up and battered as she was, she managed to maintain an air of defiance, staring straight ahead, lips tightly closed.

"Agent Marshall?" Caldwell said, standing behind her.

"The investigation's already gone public," Marshall said, her voice hoarse but steady. "There are media vans in the parking lot. Even you can't make this disappear."

Caldwell laughed softly. "My dear Agent Marshall," he said, "things have been disappearing in these caves since before you were born. Though I admit, it's been a while since we've had to dispose of a federal agent—"

He was interrupted by a man wearing tactical gear who rushed in and whispered something in Caldwell's ear. Caldwell's expression darkened. He thought for a moment, then turned again to Marshall and said, loud enough for them to hear, "It seems Detective North and his geological friend have slipped away from our little circus upstairs. But we'll get them and, perhaps when we have them, you'll be more cooperative."

"Hah! They're smarter than you think," Marshall said. "North figured out your operation days ago. The human trafficking, the money laundering, all of it."

Caldwell stepped forward, drew back his hand and... the sound of the slap echoed through the chamber. "Find them, and quickly, before this blows up in our faces," he snapped. "An hour. Find them within the hour, or we collapse the entire western section. My father's methods may have been crude, but they were effective."

Jack and Amelia exchanged glances. "What now?" she whispered. "The shaft continues upward, possibly to the surface, but if we leave, we leave her to..."

Jack sat back on his haunches, pulled his backup piece from its holster at his ankle and offered it to Amelia. She took it from him and slipped it into her pack, then pulled something else from her pack.

"Mining charges?" Jack asked.

"Not quite," she replied. "Not exactly standard issue, but... Well, I always carry charges for rock sampling," she whispered.

"If we can create a distraction big enough to draw off some of the guards—"

She was interrupted when an alarm began to blare through the cave system and below, one of Caldwell's men burst in.

"The FBI and SWAT," he yelled. "They just breached the northern entrance! They're coming in heavy!"

Caldwell's mask of control fell away. "What? How the hell did they—"

Jack smiled. "Kate," Jack whispered. "She must have somehow followed our trail."

And then chaos erupted below as men scrambled for weapons. Caldwell turned wildly this way and that, shouting orders, his composure gone. "Get those damn trucks moving! Now! Seal the tunnels! We have to make sure nothing can lead back to—"

The rest of his words were drowned out by an explosion, followed by the unmistakable sound of multiple flash-bangs. SWAT was moving fast.

Jack grabbed Amelia's arm. "It's now or never," he snapped.

Amelia took several of the small charges from her pack and handed them to him.

"Amelia, we don't have long," he whispered urgently. "If we let them close the tunnels, the evidence of decades of crimes will disappear forever."

"We need to prevent them from sealing them," Amelia whispered, already pulling more charges from her pack. "They'll try to collapse the main junctions first. It's what I would do."

Jack surveyed the scene below. Most of Caldwell's men were moving toward the FBI incursion, leaving only two guards with Marshall. Caldwell himself was standing at a computer terminal, typing frantically.

"Can you trigger a targeted collapse?" Jack asked. "Something to trap their vehicles without bringing the whole damn system down?"

Amelia's eyes gleamed. She grinned at him and said, "The loading bay. It's a natural choke point." She pulled her iPad from her pack and brought up a schematic of the tunnel system. "Here," she said, pointing. "If we time it right…"

"How long?" Jack asked.

"Five minutes to plant the charges. Another three to get back to Marshall."

A series of explosions echoed from the northern tunnels, closer now, followed by sporadic gunfire.

Below them, Caldwell grabbed a hand-held radio, keyed it, and barked, "I want those trucks moving! Nothing can connect back to us. And someone find that bastard North!"

Jack checked his weapon. "I'll create a diversion, try to draw some of their attention. You get to the loading bay. Go!"

"Jack…" Amelia began, her voice was filled of concern.

"I'll be all right. Five minutes," he said firmly, shifting on his haunches. "Then trigger the charges, no matter what. Understood?"

They shared a look in the darkness, volumes passing unspoken. Then Amelia nodded and, at a crouching run, she disappeared along the shaft, back toward the loading area.

Jack counted to thirty, hoping to give her time to get into position. Then he jammed both hands and forearms against the tunnel wall and kicked out the grate.

The crash of the falling iron grate echoed through the chamber below. Both guards spun around toward the sound, weapons raised as Jack dropped down behind them, taking advantage of their split second of confusion. The first guard went down gagging from a straight fingered strike to the throat. The second managed to squeeze off a shot that ricocheted off the cave wall right before Jack's elbow struck his temple, knocking him out cold.

Caldwell, taken completely by surprise, staggered back several steps from the computer, but he quickly recovered.

"Well now," Caldwell said, his hand moving toward a desk drawer. "I was hoping to run into you, Detective North."

"Hands where I can see them," Jack ordered, keeping his weapon trained on Caldwell while moving crabwise toward Marshall.

"Or what?" Caldwell snapped. "You'll shoot me? Create an even bigger scandal?" his smile was cold. "My family built this town, Detective. We own it. Even if you get out of here alive, it won't matter. Money talks, evidence disappears, and these caves will keep their secrets."

An explosion rocked the chamber; Amelia's charges detonated in the loading bay. The explosion was followed by the sound of screaming metal and falling rock.

"Nope, don't think so," Jack said, grinning at him. "Those trucks aren't going nowhere. You're done, Caldwell."

Caldwell's cocky smile vanished. "You son of a bitch. You have no idea what you've done."

"Oh, but I do. I know exactly what I've done," Jack said as he pulled a knife from his coverall pocket, flipped it open and began to cut Marshall free. "We've trapped your trucks, your evidence, and you. The FBI has the other exit covered. It's over."

"Nothing's over." Caldwell pulled a device from the drawer, a detonator. "These caves have been keeping our secrets for sixty years. They'll keep a few more."

His thumb moved toward the trigger just as another explosion lit up the tunnel behind him.

Time seemed to freeze as Caldwell's thumb moved toward the detonator button. Jack lunged forward, knowing he was going to be too late.

A single gunshot echoed through the chamber.

Caldwell's hand exploded in a blossom of red, and the detonator fell to the ground. He screamed, clutching his bloody wrist as he fell to his knees.

Jack turned to see Amelia standing in the tunnel entrance,

Jack's backup weapon in both hands, still trained steadily on Caldwell. "The next one won't be in your hand," she said calmly.

In the distance, they could hear sounds of the approaching tactical teams echoing through the tunnels, getting closer. Jack stepped forward and grabbed the detonator, still keeping his weapon trained on Caldwell.

"Stay down," he said to him. "Don't move a frickin' muscle." Then he turned again to Marshall and said, "You okay?"

She nodded, rubbing her wrists as he finished cutting her free.

"Better than my cover," she said dryly. "Six months I spent building a case on their Miami connection, all blown in one night. But... thanks."

"Your Miami connection's in those trucks," Amelia said. "Along with enough evidence to put the Caldwells away for generations." She glanced at her tablet, then looked at Jack and said, "The charges brought down just enough rock to trap their convoy. They're not going anywhere."

Caldwell laughed despite his obvious pain and the blood dripping between his fingers. "You really think this is the end? My father taught me well. Money talks. Witnesses vanish. Evidence—"

"Gets archived in three separate secure locations," Amelia interrupted him. "Including everything we just recorded." She patted her tablet. "Geology isn't my only field of expertise."

The first SWAT team led by Kate herself breached the chamber.

"You couldn't just wait for backup?" she asked, glaring at Jack, but there's a hint of pride in her voice.

She looked around, taking in the scene, Caldwell on his knees bleeding, the freed federal agent, Jack and Amelia looking like they've been through hell.

"We would have missed all the fun," he replied, grinning as he holstered his Glock. "You're just in time, Cap. There are some people who need to be rescued down there. And a whole lot of evidence in here that's not going to disappear this time."

As the tactical teams secured Caldwell and cleared the chamber, Jack turned to Amelia. "Nice shot, by the way. You have hidden talents!"

She handed him his backup piece. "I dated a marksman in grad school. I guess some skills stick with you, like riding a bicycle, as they say."

By then, Kate was already organizing the evidence teams, directing the investigation.

Agent Regis Thompson arrived a few minutes later and immediately went to his partner.

"The Caldwell empire ends tonight, Regis," she said, staring at Caldwell. There was steel in her voice despite her injuries.

Jack listened, nodding slightly to himself, but he was not so sure. He watched as Caldwell was led away, the man's eyes burning with hatred. Jack shook his head, something was telling him it wasn't over. Not by a long shot.

"Let's get out of here," he said to Amelia. "I don't know about you, but I'm starving."

She nodded, "Me, too. Where?"

He looked at his watch. "There's a Chick-fil-A just up the road a piece. That work for you?"

"Sounds good," she said.

As they walked together out of the cave entrance into cool night air, Jack's phone buzzed in his pocket.

He took it out, opened the message, and... "What the hell?" he muttered.

"What? What is it?" Amelia asked.

He showed her the screen.

Well done, detective. Now I suggest you check the Old County Hospital records. You'll find something there that will interest you.

Back at the command center, after a spicy chicken sandwich and a cup of black coffee, Jack and Amelia were compiling their reports, the strange text all but forgotten. He was about to close out his report when his phone rang. He checked the screen: unknown number.

He frowned, then, on the fourth ring, he answered it. "Detective North. You've been quite busy." There was something familiar about the voice. "Perhaps it's time we discussed your grandfather's legacy. Lookout Point. Midnight. Come alone." The caller hung up, leaving Jack staring at the screen.

"Morton?" he said, frowning even more deeply.

He looked at Amelia. "That was retired Detective James Morton. He worked with my grandfather. He wants me to meet him at Lookout Point at midnight. Something about my father's legacy.

"No!" Amelia snapped, looking up from her surveillance feeds. "Absolutely not! It's too exposed. Perfect place for an ambush."

"But if Morton knows something about Charlie's investigation. Something he's been holding back—"

"Then let us set up surveillance, tactical support—"

"No," Jack said, checking his weapon. "Whoever's pulling strings will be watching. One sign of backup, and Morton will be long gone."

"Jack, you can't..." Amelia's voice carries concern born of everything they'd uncovered. "You know this is a trap."

"Probably." He said tucking his notebook into his jacket pocket. "But sometimes you have to spring the trap to catch whatever's inside."

CHAPTER 20

Monday Night

MIDNIGHT

ON A CLEAR DAY, Lookout Point at midnight is, perhaps, one of the most beautiful spots in the nation. The lights of Chattanooga sparkle below like fallen stars and the Tennessee River winds its way through the city like a ribbon of silver. On a not so nice day, as was that Monday evening when Jack parked his unmarked car behind a thick stand of rhododendrons, a quarter-mile back where the access road curved southward, storm clouds gathered over Lookout Mountain like a gray wet blanket.

Despite Amelia's protests that, "This has trap written all over it," he approached the rendezvous' alone, keeping to the shadows, every nerve in his body tingling.

His phone vibrated, breaking the silence. It was another text, "The old observation platform. Two minutes." Jack stared at it. He bit his lip. Took a deep breath and made his way to the platform.

The wooden platform was fenced off with danger signs posted at both ends and in the middle. The gate was open, the lock and chain on the floor near one of the posts.

The platform, once a tourist attraction in and of itself, extended thirty feet out over the edge of the cliff and a drop of several hundred feet. The weathered boards creaked softly as Jack stepped onto them. Morton stood at the railing, silhouetted against the night sky, both hands grasping the top rail.

"You're sailing into dangerous waters, Detective," Morton said without turning, his voice low. He sounded weary, as if he was carrying the weight of the world on his shoulders.

"Your grandfather tried the same thing back in the day," he continued. "He found connections between the Caldwells and just about every power structure in the city. Police, sheriff, politicians, even the churches—all of it tied together with blood and money."

"Before the cancer took him," Jack said quietly. "He never stopped trying to prove it, though, did he? Even in hospice, he kept working."

Morton snorted. "Eight years gone," he said, his voice filled with irony, "and his case notes still make more sense than most active investigations." Morton's grip on the railing tightened until his knuckles whitened. "He wasn't the first cop, you know, to notice the pattern. Three others tried in the sixties. But Charlie... he was the first to follow the money instead of the bodies. He started mapping the foundations, the shell companies, but got too close."

A twig snapped in the darkness behind them; too sharp to be wildlife. Jack spun around, his weapon drawn, his tactical light cutting through shadows.

Morton didn't move.

"We're not alone," he said calmly. "Haven't been since you arrived. They're very good at watching, Caldwell's people. And so they should be. They've been doing it for generations."

Out of the shadows, six figures materialized against the tree line, six men in tactical gear, weapons raised, moving with military precision. Behind them, Edwin Caldwell walked slowly forward. The mountain air seemingly invigorating the man rather than burdening his eighty-three years. His cane tapped against the stone footpath, the sound echoing across the valley.

He stopped just inside the fence, the six men in a semi-circle behind him.

"Detective North," the old man's voice was cultured, the voice of old money. "I believe it's time we discussed your grandfather's legacy. Charlie was an excellent investigator. Shame about the cancer. Though if he hadn't gotten sick, well…" He stepped onto the platform and tapped his cane meaningfully against the boards. "Other arrangements might have been necessary."

Jack glared at him, his weapon pointed at the old man's chest, but said nothing.

"Your grandfather's investigation went deeper than anyone knew," Caldwell continued, positioning himself carefully.

Jack took two steps sideways, keeping Caldwell between him and his men.

"He mapped the entire operation, the foundations, the offshore accounts, the political connections. He even found caves we thought were safely hidden. Caves that held… particular interests."

Jack kept his weapon trained on the old man, noting his men's equipment, body armor, modified M4 carbines, thermal imaging. *Not regular security*, he thought. These men were professional wetwork specialists.

"And you let him live?" Jack asked, an edge to his voice. "Sloppy of you, wasn't it?"

Caldwell shrugged. "He had no actual proof. Cancer was a convenient solution." Caldwell smiled coldly. "No questions asked. No loose ends. Perfectly natural causes. Though I must admit, watching him spend his final years trying to prove what no one would believe… Well, that was its own kind of justice. Watching him fade while his evidence gathered dust. Poetry, really."

"Oh, he left proof," Morton interjected, his hand moving slowly toward his jacket. "He had insurance. I've been holding it since before he got sick. Waiting for the right moment."

"And yet here we are, Detective," Caldwell waved his free hand, gesturing expansively to the city below. "Eight years later, still standing. Your grandfather died knowing he'd failed. Just like you will."

"We found something interesting in those truck manifests," Agent Marshall's voice cut through the night air as she emerged from the shadows, weapon trained, her FBI team moving into position behind her. "Proof of everything he tried to expose. Names that go all the way to Washington."

More figures appeared: Amelia with a rifle trained on one of Caldwell's men, Kate's SWAT members, securing the perimeter. They'd planned for just such a scenario as this, letting Jack play bait while positioning their forces.

But for some reason, Caldwell didn't seem too bothered. "Nice one, Detective," he said. "But your grandfather was right about one thing," Caldwell's voice carried a new edge. "The caves go deeper than anyone knows." He raised his cane, moonlight glinting off the red button on its handle. "Care to see how deep?"

"The platform's rigged," Amelia shouted through Jack's earpiece. "Thermal imaging shows there are charges on the support beams."

"Again with the explosives?" Jack said sarcastically. "Your son tried that, and it didn't work for him."

Caldwell shrugged. "We're miners, so why not?" Caldwell smiled, his confidence unshaken despite being surrounded. "Insurance. Like your grandfather thought he had." His finger hovered over the button. "I'm going to leave now. You're going to stay exactly where you are. This detonator has a range of almost a thousand feet. One press, and we all get a very long look at the caves below. Rather fitting, don't you think? Dying where it all started?"

"You're surrounded," Jack said as he stepped slowly forward. "It's over."

"Nothing's over. The foundations will continue. The work will go on." Caldwell's eyes gleamed in the light of a dozen or more tactical flashlights. "Your grandfather died knowing he couldn't stop us. He spent his last days obsessing over proof no one would believe. Such a waste of a brilliant mind."

"Except he did leave proof," Morton shouted as he pulled a thumb drive from his inside jacket pocket. "Everything's here. Everything Charlie documented. Every connection. Every crime."

"You think?" Caldwell asked, his composure flagging slightly. "Where's the rest of it?"

"The rest of it?" Jack studied the old man's reaction.

"The other evidence. The cave surveys. He found something in those caves, something he shouldn't, something that scared him more than dying. Where is it?"

"Drop the cane, Caldwell." Jack took another step closer, watching his thumb on the detonator. "Maybe we can figure it out together—"

Caldwell sprang forward with startling speed, lunging forward, the cane arcing through the air toward Jack. Jack intercepted it mid-swing, grappling with Caldwell at the platform's edge. The old man was surprisingly strong, or was it just the adrenaline coursing through his body that lent power to his aging muscles?

"Your grandfather died a failure," Caldwell snarled, struggling for control of the cane. "Rambling about caves and conspiracies. No one believed him then. No one will believe you now."

Marshall moved forward to help Jack, but she couldn't get a clear angle with Caldwell and Jack struggling for the cane. Her tactical team held their position, weapons trained but unable to risk a shot with Jack so close to the edge. The old boards creaked ominously beneath their feet as the two men fought for control of the cane.

"He died knowing the truth would come out," Jack growled through clenched teeth, using his leverage to keep the button away from Caldwell's reaching thumb. "He knew that someone would finish what he started."

It was at that moment that the rain began to fall, making the wooden boards slippery and treacherous.

Morton, now with his back to the rail, turned his head and stared downward beyond the railing where the cliff dropped away into darkness. Lightning flashed overhead, illuminating the desperation on Caldwell's face.

"You insolent little whelp," he snarled, twisting the cane with surprising agility, his fingers now only inches from the button. "You think you can do what your betters couldn't? Your grandfather found only the surface, the trafficking, the money, yes, but beyond that—" His eyes took on a maniacal gleam.

"Show him, Jack," Morton yelled. "Show him what Charlie really left behind."

With an almighty wrench, Jack tore the cane from the old man's hands and staggered backward to crash into the rail. The rail cracked, but held.

Caldwell, now on his back on the boards, rolled over, scrambled to his knees and, with an effort, hauled himself to his feet.

Jack, cane in one hand, his phone in the other, came forward and shoved the phone in Caldwell's face. "See?" he said. "See what he had, what we now have?"

The screen was showing Caldwell a list of cave mapping overlays matched with foundation records. The old man's eyes widened in recognition.

"Impossible," he whispered. "Those surveys were destroyed. I watched them burn."

"Charlie made copies," Jack said, his attention fully now on

Caldwell. His face so close to his he could feel the old man's breath. "He hid them where only another detective would think to look for them. In plain sight. Game over, Mr. Caldwell."

The old man's face contorted with rage. He made a wild grab for the cane. Jack, taken unawares, lost his grip and Caldwell, with a strength born of desperation, slammed his thumb down on the button. Lightning flashed. Thunder crashed overhead.

Marshall launched herself forward, grabbed Jack's arm and, with a supreme burst of energy, flung Jack sideways off the platform. Jack hit the ground hard, the breath forced out of his lungs.

And... then... nothing!

"Looking for this?" Amelia crawled out from under the platform, soaked to the skin, holding up a small electronic device.

"Detonator receiver," she said breathlessly. "Disabled. My grandfather's notes were very specific about your failsafes, Mr. Caldwell."

All the fight drained out of the old man and, for the first time, as FBI agents moved in to secure him and his tactical team, he looked his age.

The rain intensified, the thunder and lighting increased.

"Your grandfather would have enjoyed this moment," Morton said as they led Caldwell away toward the waiting vehicles. "He made me promise to hold onto this until someone was ready to finish what he started. Someone smart enough to see the patterns. Someone stubborn enough to follow them through," he said as he pulled a worn leather notebook from inside his jacket, protected from the rain by a plastic Ziplock bag. "Charlie knew he was dying," he continued, "but he loved you, Jack, so I'm glad it's you."

Jack took the notebook from him, feeling its weight, not just the paper and leather, but the years of investigation and determination in the face of death.

"There's a lot there, Jack," Morton said. "He made detailed maps, financial records, names, some of whom are still in power in Chattanooga. And there's something else, coordinates to cave systems that don't appear on any of the official surveys."

"There's more," Marshall said as she approached, water streaming from her tactical gear. "Caldwell's phone shows there are locations across three states, Tennessee, Alabama and Georgia. The operation goes deeper than we thought."

"And the foundations are still active," Amelia added, as she joined them. "There are other family members involved. Old man Caldwell is just one head of the hydra."

Jack slipped his father's notebook inside the inner pocket of his rain jacket.

"Then we keep digging until we get 'em all," he said.

His phone buzzed in his pocket. He took it out and looked at the screen. It was a text from an unknown number: "Your grandfather's maps just scratched the surface. Want to see how deep the caves really go?"

Morton read the message over his shoulder, rain dripping from his silver hair. "Another trap?"

"Probably," Jack said, watching the federal agents load Caldwell into an armored transport. "But grandad never stopped looking for the truth and neither will I."

CHAPTER 21

Tuesday Morning

FBI COMMAND CENTER
  Kate
  8am

IT WAS at that point I joined the group at the platform. It had been quite a night, and not just because of what had happened in the caves and at the platform at Lookout Point. It was the weather. I've known storms in the past, but nothing quite like that one on the top of the mountain that night. The platform is almost twenty-five hundred feet above the city and it was awash. The skies had opened and the noise of the thunder crackling seemingly only a few hundred feet above our heads... It couldn't have been much worse in the trenches during the Battle of the Somme in 1916. And, as I joined the group, it seemed to get worse. Thunder cracked overhead, lightning lit up the mountain-top. Was it an omen of things yet to come? I didn't know. What I did know was that the investigation was far from over. And what

I was worried about was Jack. Exactly how and why I couldn't tell you; I just knew I was.

"Captain," Jack said as I joined him, Amelia Croft, Detective Morton, and Agent Marshall.

"Your grandfather would be proud of you, Jack," I said as we watched Caldwell's vehicle pull away. "He started this fight. Now we finish it. You up for it?"

A clap of thunder rolled across the mountain as if to punctuate the question.

He nodded, grinning, then said, "You know it, Kate!"

"Better get some rest then," I said. "It looks like it will be a busy day tomorrow."

I looked at my watch. It was just after one o'clock. It was already tomorrow.

But, so he told me, Jack didn't get much sleep that night. He arrived home at just after one-thirty, took a quick hot shower, set an alarm on his phone for six-thirty and then fell into bed.

According to him, he awoke four and a half hours later to the sound of raucous music; his alarm. He literally fell out of bed, grabbed his phone from the bedside table, fumbled with it, getting more desperate by the second until, at last, he managed to turn it off.

An hour later, by seven-thirty, he was on the road, and by eight that morning he was in the FBI command center sitting at a conference table studying his father's notebook, now supplemented by copies of the original investigation, also supplied by Morton.

Me? I'd been there an hour when he arrived. I sat down at the table opposite him.

The command center was buzzing with activity as evidence teams processed items we'd seized from Forrest's Cave while Agent Marshall was coordinating with the Miami field office on the human trafficking angle.

Amelia, too, had had a rough night, so she said, but she'd

somehow managed to arrive at the command center some fifteen minutes earlier than Jack.

"Look at this," she said as she spread a cave survey across the table. "The coordinates in your grandfather's notebook; they don't match any official mining records, but they do align with the property holdings of three major Caldwell foundations."

"And these," Sarah Marshall said as she sat down beside him, iPad in hand, "are your grandfather's medical records and, from what I can tell, every one of the doctors that handled his treatment had connections to at least one of the Caldwell foundations."

Jack took the tablet from her and flipped quickly through the screens, then he flipped back again, then he flipped through them more slowly.

"This one," he said finally, holding the iPad so Marshall could see. "Dr. Victoria Hayes, Head of Oncology. Charlie mentioned her in his notes. She was his oncologist. She was treating him."

His phone buzzed; another unknown number: "Ready to see what really happened in those treatment rooms? Old County Hospital, basement level. The morgue keeps interesting records."

He reached across the table and showed it to me. "What d'you think?" he asked. "I don't think it's Morton."

"I think it's another trap," I replied.

"The old County Hospital? Isn't that at the foot of the mountain in St Elmo?" Amelia asked, reading over his shoulder. "It's been abandoned for years"

"Not entirely," Marshall said, pulling up the old hospital's utility records. "Look. There's still power to it, and it's being consumed. It looks like there are environmental controls running."

"Let me see those maps," Amelia said, reaching around Jack and across the table. "Your grandfather's. Where are they?"

Jack riffled through a pile of maps, found what he was looking for and dragged it out and laid it out in front of her. "This what you're looking for?" he asked.

Amelia studied it for a moment, then said, "Yes. Look. Here's the hospital… And see here? See what your grandfather did? These lines… They represent tunnels. They connect the hospital to the cave system. Your grandfather mapped it out."

Jack leaned back in his chair, his arms folded across his chest. He stared at the map, frowning. "Why?" he asked. "Why would they connect the hospital to the caves?"

"Are you kidding?" Amelia asked. "If what you say is true, there could be as many as sixty dead bodies in those caves. Think how many live ones they must have transported through the system. It would make sense for them to have some sort of… medical division. Someone had to look after the trafficees, wouldn't they? And develop… God only knows what."

"Like engineered cancer?" Jack's voice had an edge to it. "Three times she ordered a new 'experimental therapy' for him. I think maybe she killed him. "

"But who killed who?" I asked.

Jack looked up at me and said, "I think they killed Charlie, my grandfather. I think we need to take a look at that hospital."

I looked skeptically at him. "Amelia's right. That old place has been shut down for almost twenty-five years…" I looked at Marshall. "The power's on, you say?"

Marshall nodded.

"Why would the power be on?" I wondered, out loud.

"Hayes was head of oncology there. She was my father's doctor. I think maybe she, when my grandfather got too close… I think she killed him. And, on thinking about it, I think she was conducting experiments on him. Look, the power's on in that hospital. That means something, right? And, according to my grandfather's maps, the place is connected to caves. I say we take a look."

I stood up and stared down at the map. *It's supposed to be aban-*

doned, I thought, *but the power's on. Why? That's probable cause enough to...* "Let's do it—"

"Now wait just a minute," SAIC Thompson said from behind Marshall. "I heard all that and I don't like this any more than you do but—"

"Sorry, Regis," I said. "We've come too far for you guys to step in and take the credit. You can tag along, if you like, but my chief insists we take the lead. You in, or what?"

Thompson took a deep breath, glared at me, then grinned and said, "You know I have the authority to overrule your chief and take it over and..." he thought for a second or two, then nodded and said, "Okay. You take the lead, but we'll be right there with you." He looked at Sarah and said, "Marshall, you're up. Don't let 'em screw it up."

CHAPTER 22

Tuesday

Old County Hospital
Kate
10am

AN HOUR LATER, Jack told me, he and Amelia were in Jack's unmarked car in the lot of what once had been a busy hospital, waiting for me and my team to show up. I arrived only moments after he did and parked next to him and rolled my window down. The place looked dilapidated, deserted, with broken windows, the parking lot cracked, with weeds growing up through gaps. It was a dreary-looking place. *But is the dilapidation merely a facade?* I wondered.

"Security cameras," Jack said, leaning across Amelia to the open car window. "They look... They're not old. Hmm... I'm going to take a look around the back."

"Be careful," I said, "and stay out of sight."

He nodded, put the car in drive and slowly circled the massive building.

The hospital lot had been partially carved out of the side of the mountain, thus the access area at the back of the building was narrow, perhaps twenty yards from wall to cliff.

According to Jack, as they circumnavigated the south side of the building, he slowed the car to a crawl. Then, as they rounded the corner into the rear access area, he pulled sharply over to the left, almost to the wall, and stopped the car.

"Look," he said to Amelia, "all the way down there. I can see at least three vehicles at the loading docks. Who are they, and what the hell are they doing?"

"Looks like they're clearing stuff out of there," Amelia said. "What are we going to do?"

Jack put the car in reverse and reversed back around the corner of the building and then turned the car around and returned to the front of the building where I was studying the building schematics on the hood of my car with Agent Sarah Marshall at my side and three blue and white cruisers parked nearby along with Marshall's SUV.

Jack parked beside my unmarked cruiser, exited the vehicle, joined me at the hood, and said, "There are at least three trucks around back. It looks like they're on the move, whoever they are. What d'you want to do, Kate?"

I straightened up, turned to look at him and said, "Do we actually know what they're doing? Could they be legit?"

Jack looked skeptically at me. "You're kidding, right? This place is supposed to be abandoned. They shouldn't even be here. Let's go round 'em up."

"You don't know that, Jack," I replied. "They could, and probably do, have a legitimate reason to be doing what they're doing. Someone owns this place. That means someone could have sent them to... Hell, I don't know, but we can't go arresting people without cause. You know that. Now, take it easy while I try to figure this thing out. Hey, Jackson. C'mere," I shouted to one of the uniformed officers. "There are several trucks round the back of the building. I want to know what they're doing. Take Harvey with you. Keep an eye on them and keep out of sight."

Officer Jackson nodded, turned and ran back to his car. I turned again to the schematic. "The main entrance is sealed," I said, "but it looks like there's an emergency exit door here at the end of the old morgue delivery tunnel. Your grandfather noted it in his files, Jack."

"They won't expect us through that route," Amelia said. "If we move now…"

"Don't we need a warrant?" Jack asked sarcastically, then frowned as his phone buzzed again. He swiped the screen and read the message. *"Better hurry, Detective. They're removing the records."*

"Who the hell…?" Jack said, showing me the phone.

Marshall instinctively checked her weapon, then said, "I'll call it in and coordinate some tactical support. After what happened at the cave, we go in heavy."

"Wait," Amelia interrupted her, studying her laptop on the hood of Jack's car. "I've hacked into the power system. These readings. They're not right. Something's going on in there. Whatever's in there, it's not just paperwork."

I could see Jack was deep in thought. I learned later he was thinking about his grandfather's final days. The old man had died at home. Jack hadn't seen much of him those last few years, but he had been there when he died. The old man had never mentioned his investigation, not even to his detective grandson. It was something Jack had never thought about, not until a week earlier when I'd dropped the case on him, but now he couldn't get his grandfather out of his head.

"Research!" he snapped. "Hayes isn't just running. She's protecting her research. They must be into something bad."

I looked at him. "If what you say is true, we can't go in there. We're going to need to call in the CDC before—"

"There's no time for that," Jack snapped. "If we wait, there'll be nothing left. We have to go in now."

"But Jack, we can't," I said. "If Hayes is half as smart as your grandfather's notes suggest—"

"She'll be ready for us," Jack finished for me. "So, forewarned is forearmed. We need to go in now."

"One more thing," Marshall said, bringing up personnel files. "I've been running Hayes' background. She has surgical privileges at every major hospital in the region. Perfect cover for monitoring test subjects. Look, here she is with the Caldwells."

She held up her iPad for us to see.

"Test subjects," Jack muttered angrily. "Like my granddad." He looked at the photo of Hayes at a Caldwell Foundation event. She was standing between Edwin and Richard Caldwell, all three smiling at the camera. "She didn't just treat him. She watched him die," he said bitterly.

My radio crackled and came to life. It was Jackson. "There's movement at the loading docks. Multiple SUVs, and staff in medical scrubs."

"Scrubs at an abandoned hospital?" Marshall said, frowning as she checked her vest. "They're not even trying to be subtle anymore."

"They're getting ready to move out," Jack said, tucking his grandfather's notebook into his vest. "With both Caldwells in custody, Hayes has to protect their research. Whatever's in that morgue... It's what she used to kill him."

I nodded. "Get yourselves ready," I snapped, and five minutes later with my teams in position, I said into the radio. "We breach on my signal."

I watched as Jack checked his weapon one last time. I looked up at the old hospital's dark walls and windows that towered above the empty lot and inwardly I shuddered. "Somewhere in there lay the answers to Charlie North's death and so much more… along with whoever was sending Jack those messages."

"Go, go, go," I snapped into the radio and together with Jack, Amelia and four uniformed officers in tactical gear, we ran to the old morgue emergency exit on the north side of the hospital while Marshall's FBI team were covering the perimeter.

"That padlock looks new," Jack said.

"Let me," Amelia said, reaching into her bag.

Jack and I stared at the rusted steel door as Amelia worked on the lock. "Where did you learn that?" he asked as she worked her picks.

"Lessons of a misspent youth," she muttered through her teeth.

"Damn," he said as the lock clicked open. "You never cease to amaze."

She smiled at him. "You have no idea, Detective," she replied, smiling at him.

"All right. That's enough," I said. "Let's do this." And I grabbed the doorknob, turned it and pulled the door outward. It opened with a shrill shriek of protesting metal.

Beyond the door, a wide passage way stretched away into darkness. We stepped inside. I frowned. The air was cold and… I sniffed the air. "Antiseptics," I whispered.

"Hayes is here somewhere," Jack said as he started along the passageway, Glock in hand, the beam of his tactical light cutting through the darkness. "It's time we shut her and her research program down. Permanently."

"Pressure door," Amelia whispered, her light catching a metal door. "See? That's an environmental seal. They've modified the old morgue infrastructure."

Jack studied the door. "New keypad," he said. "But look, they kept the manual override." He pointed to a small lever to the left of the door. "I wonder why. More to the point, I wonder if it still works."

He grasped the small lever and pushed it upward. At first it didn't move, but then, with a tiny squeak, it yielded, and the heavy door opened onto a steel-lined corridor, the floor polished to a mirror shine beneath a fine layer of dust.

I looked for footprints. There were none. "Keep going," I said.

"Thermal imaging is showing multiple contacts in the loading dock area," Marshall's voice came through our earpieces. "They're moving equipment out."

"The temperature's dropping," Amelia said. "Look. They're operating some sort of cold storage."

She was right. There were literally dozens of modern freezer units set against the walls, side-by-side, one after another, their displays lit up showing controlled temperatures and, through the reinforced windows, I could see racks of carefully labeled samples.

"Movement ahead," Marshall warned. "I mark three heat signatures approaching your position."

"Quick, in here," I snapped. It was a rush, but we made it just in time, all seven of us. We ducked into a side room and, through the crack in the door, I watched as three technicians in full containment gear wheeled a cart past our position. The containers on it were also marked with biohazard symbols.

The footsteps faded but, as we stepped out into the corridor, somewhere deeper inside the facility, I could hear the hum of machinery.

Amelia went to one of the freezer units and looked through the glass. "Hey," she whispered urgently. "These storage units... they're not just for keeping samples. They're actually producing something."

"We don't have time for that now," I snapped. "We have to keep moving. Come on."

We followed the corridor deeper into the facility, passing more storage units along the way, each humming with active cooling systems, past door after door on either side. Through the glass panels, we could see laboratories that should have had no place in an abandoned hospital: state-of-the-art equipment, computer systems, testing stations.

"What the hell is going on here?" I muttered.

"Well, it isn't just storage, that's for sure," Amelia whispered. "It's some kind of production facility. They're manufacturing something. God only knows what."

"Multiple subjects," Marshall snapped through the comms. "I count at least twenty active workstations. They've been busy."

"Copy that," I said. "We're moving on."

And we did, until we reached a door at the end of the hallway with a plaque thereon that carried a familiar name: DR. VICTORIA HAYES - RESEARCH DIRECTOR. I took a step back. I could see light under the door.

I edged closer, with Jack at my side. We could hear voices within. We could clearly hear a woman's voice which I took to be Hayes:

"...need everything transferred before morning," she said. "The Caldwells' arrest changes nothing. The research continues."

"But the FBI—" another voice protested; a man's this time.

"They won't find anything," the woman interrupted him. "They'll be too late. North's grandson may have his grandfather's persistence, but he lacks the scientific background to understand what he's seeing. By the time he figures it out..."

I took a step back and motioned two of the uniformed officers forward, then, to them and the others, I raised three fingers to countdown to the breach. But before I could begin, an alarm blared throughout the facility.

"Containment breach in Sector six," an automated voice announced. "Emergency protocols initiated." And the warning kept repeating.

Red lights came on all along the hallway and, from somewhere nearby, I could hear the hiss of releasing gas.

"Gas!" Amelia snapped. "It's some kind of aerosol dispersal through the ventilation system."

"All teams, masks!" Marshall orders through comms. "I'm contacting HAZMAT. We need containment protocols now!"

"We've got to get out of here, now!" Jack yelled.

The red emergency lights cast eerie shadows as a gray mist covered the floor.

Through Hayes' door, they hear her issuing instructions: "Seal the research wing. Let's observe the detective's response. Like grandfather, like grandson."

"Options?" I snapped.

Amelia dragged her laptop from her bag and opened it, balancing it on her left arm.

"I'm still in," she whispered as her fingers flew across the keys. "Your grandfather's notes, Jack. Look. He made notes of the environmental control override codes. The original hospital systems must still be in place, right?"

"How long?" I snapped.

"I need two minutes to access the master controls. But I need to reach the main utility junction."

"Which is where?" I snapped.

Amelia pulled up the schematics. "Maintenance room, back down the corridor. Through the old autopsy suite. Come on." And she turned and began to run, her laptop still in the crook of her arm.

"I can hear you," Hayes called through the door. "You won't make it. It's already beginning." Then she laughed and shouted, "Perhaps you'd like to discuss treatment options?"

"I'll see you in hell," Jack shouted as we turned and ran.

The mist was up to our ankles, thick, almost viscous, swirling around our feet as we ran, following Amelia's directions to the old autopsy suite. Behind them, Hayes' voice carried over the facility's speaker system.

"Fascinating, isn't it? Watching the exposure begin. Your

grandfather showed similar initial symptoms - elevated heart rate, respiratory distress. We documented everything, as we are documenting them now."

"Through here," Amelia shouted as she stopped at a heavy steel door, grabbed the handle, turned it and pushed. The door opened inward. The autopsy suite beyond was a merger of old and new, the original tile walls lined with modern monitoring equipment. Steel tables gleaming under the emergency lighting.

"I mark multiple signatures converging on your position," Marshall warned. "They're trying to box you in."

Jack told me later it was at that point his vision blurred, but he shook his head.

Me, I felt nothing.

"The utility junction?" I snapped. "Where is it?"

"There should be an access panel behind that storage unit," Amelia said, putting her laptop down and reaching for the unit.

"Let me," Jack said. And he grabbed the unit and, with an almighty effort, dragged the unit to one side.

"Cover me," Amelia snapped. "This will take a minute."

Hayes' voice echoed through the speaker system, "The aggression should begin soon. Fight or flight response, heightened by our targeted agents. Your grandfather became quite agitated in this phase. The video records were... enlightening."

It was then I heard running footsteps out in the corridor. I ordered my four uniformed officers to guard the door.

"Shove that table across the door," I said, pointing to a large steel autopsy table. "It won't hold them long but it should buy us some time."

The mist was by then up to our calves.

"How much longer?" I called to Amelia as Jack and I took up a defensive position just beyond the officers with our weapons drawn.

"I'm almost... Wait. There's something wrong. The controls aren't responding like they should."

It was Hayes' voice that answered her. "Did you really think we wouldn't modify the original systems? Your grandfather's notes are outdated, Detective. Like his research. Like his efforts to expose us. Not long now. Breath deeply. It will be over soon."

"Keep trying, Amelia," Jack yelled. "Charlie wouldn't have left us hanging." He pulled out the old notebook and flipped desperately through the pages.

Hayes' voice floats through the speakers: "Confusion setting in? It's perfectly normal at this stage. Your grandfather's cognitive decline was particularly well-documented."

But Jack found what he was looking for - a page he'd nearly missed before. "Amelia! There's another panel. The utility junction. There's an older access point. It should be there, behind that one. Out of the way. Let me get at it."

With Hayes' people now banging on the door, Jack and Amelia struggled to move the last cabinet.

"Whatever you're doing—"

"Got it!" Amelia shouted triumphantly as she found the hatch and pried it open to reveal the original hospital systems. She stared at the controls, controls that haven't seen the light in decades.

"What are you..." Hayes' voice wavered slightly. "That system was supposed to have been sealed before—"

"Before you killed my grandfather?" Jack shouted. "But he found it. And he left it for someone smart enough to follow his trail."

Amelia, her bottom lip firmly between her teeth, her brow furrowed, eyes narrowed, flipped switch after switch until, at last, the ventilation system roared into life. Not the modern units Hayes controlled, but the original hospital system, designed to handle 1960s containment protocols. The mist began to clear as the backup generators kicked in to handle the drain on the power systems.

"No!" Hayes sounded as if she was close to panic. "No! No! No! Seal all sectors! Release the secondary agents!"

But Amelia was already ahead of her. Standing at the table, at her laptop, still inside the hospital computer system, she set about locking down Hayes' systems. "I don't think so, Doctor," she uttered as her fingers flew over the keys. "Not this time."

"Let's get the hell out of here," a voice outside the door shouted. And the assault on the door stopped. All was quiet, except for the sound of running footsteps fading into the distance.

The red emergency lights still pulsed, but the air was clearing, the mist around our feet thinning as the old ventilation system sucked whatever the crap was out.

"Get that table out of the way," I snapped. "I want Hayes."

The officers dragged the table away from the door and we ran out into the corridor, turned left and ran back to Hayes' door just as it crashed open. She emerged with two men. She was wearing a white lab coat, the two men tactical gear and they were armed with what appeared to be assault weapons. All three were wearing sophisticated breathing apparatus. She took her breather off and glared at us. To say she didn't look happy would be an understatement. She was livid.

"HAZMAT team is on the way. All areas and combatants secured." Marshall stated through the comms.

"Do you have any idea what you've done?" Hayes shouted. "Years of research, perfect delivery systems, untraceable methods—"

"Like the one you used on my grandfather?" Jack advanced on her despite his lingering symptoms. "You used him. You experimented on him, and you killed him."

"Your grandfather was a triumph of targeted pathology," Hayes snapped. "Every stage of his demise was documented, every reaction measured. His death advanced our work by decades. And now...." She nodded to her guards.

They looked at her, then at my officers, and slowly they raised their left hands and lowered their weapons to the floor. It was over.

"Victoria Hayes," I said. "You're under arrest for the murder of Charles North, Mary Ellen Grimes and God knows how many others."

"Murder?" Hayes actually laughed. "I did no such thing. I advanced medical science. Perfected delivery methods that governments only dreamed of. Ask your superiors, Agent Marshall. Ask them who really funded our research. And besides, I had nothing to do with the death of any Grimes person."

"Found something," Amelia called from Hayes' office. "Records of her test subjects. Everything. Names, dates... connections to federal agencies."

"It's over, Doctor," Jack said. "Time to answer for what you did to my grandfather."

Hayes straightened her lab coat, her professional composure returning. "Your grandfather understood the science, Detective. He saw the potential. He just couldn't accept the necessity of progress." She held out her wrists for Jack's cuffs. "Some minds are too small to see the larger picture."

"Progress?" Jack said as he snapped the cuffs over her wrists. "You murdered people. That's not progress."

"We advanced human evolution," she replied with clinical detachment. "Every subject, including your grandfather, contributed to something greater than themselves. Though I must admit, Charles was special."

"Jack, Captain Gazzara," Amelia said. She was still in Hayes' office. "These weren't just experiments. Look at the funding sources. Military contracts, intelligence agencies..."

"Black budget research," Marshall said as she joined us. "Engineered bio-weapons, Doctor?" she asked.

Hayes stared at the FBI initials emblazoned on her jacket, but she didn't answer.

"The Caldwells provided the infrastructure, didn't they?" Marshall asked. "But you, Hayes... You, Hayes, you were the real weapon."

Hayes looked at them with something like pride. For a moment she said nothing, and then, "Your grandfather's last days were his most useful. The way the cancer progressed, how it responded to each modification... pure scientific poetry."

"That's enough," Jack snapped, but Hayes continued.

"He knew, you see. He knew he was dying, but he kept investigating even as the cancer ate through him. What a man he was. Such determination. And it's genetic, apparently." She tilted her head to one side and studied Jack with what looked to me like clinical interest. "Though I'm curious... I think you'd better have your bloodwork checked. You never know... and after our little exposure test. Well, some agents take time to manifest. You'll be sure to let me know how it goes, won't you, Detective?"

"Save it for the federal prosecutors, Doctor," Marshall said as she nodded to two of her agents. "I'm sure they'll be fascinated by your research."

As we watched them lead her away, Amelia grabbed Jack's arm and said, "She's bluffing, Jack. The ventilation system cleared it all away before it could take hold."

I went into her office and looked around. It was going to take days to clear and catalogue the decades of research, test subjects, and... the connections to people in power. Some of the names I knew quite well, some I didn't know at all. "This goes way deeper than we thought," I muttered to myself. *And who the hell was it that was messaging Jack?* I thought. *And where the hell are they?*

I'd been expecting to find that particular someone somewhere in the building, but we didn't. And, just as that thought entered my mind, Jack's phone buzzed.

He tapped the screen and opened the message. *Well done Detective. Hayes was just the beginning. Are you ready to learn who really ordered your grandfather's death?*

CHAPTER 23

Tuesday afternoon

COMMAND CENTER
Jack
2pm

BY TWO O'CLOCK THAT AFTERNOON, Kate and Sarah Marshall had wrapped things up at old County Hospital and the FBI evidence team was already boxing up Hayes' records and transferring them to the command center.

Kate Gazzara had gone back to the police department, leaving Jack with instructions to wrap things up and write a full report. He was also to ignore further texts from what appeared to be his anonymous benefactor, including the one he'd just received. But Jack... well, Jack being Jack never was one to take such instructions seriously, was he?

The command center that afternoon resembled a war room. Evidence from the old County Hospital covered every flat surface while a team of analysts processed Hayes' records. The

HAZMAT team was still at the hospital, and would be for several days, securing the biological agents while Marshall coordinated the federal agencies, including the CDC who by then also had a team at the hospital.

"The initial analysis confirms there were forty-seven victims," Marshall said to Jack as she sat down beside him. "All diagnosed with 'natural' conditions. All treated by Hayes during her research."

She put a hand on his arm. "You should get yourself checked out, Jack," she said when she saw him rubbing his temples. "After that exposure in the morgue…"

"I already did," he replied. "Bloodwork's clear. I'm good."

He nodded to Amelia who was poring over several documents spread out on the conference table. "She never quits, does she?" He said, more to himself than to Marshall.

"Well, if you're sure you're okay," she said, rising to her feet.

"Yeah, I'm good. Really, but thanks."

She nodded, then turned and walked to join her boss at a table at the far end of the room.

Jack sat for a moment staring at Amelia, then he too rose to his feet and went to join Amelia.

"Three more facilities like Hayes', all with government contracts. All using the caves as a collection point," she said, looking up at him.

Jack's phone buzzed again. He looked at Amelia. She raised her eyebrows and nodded.

Jack flipped the screen and opened the message. *Time's running out, Detective. Your grandfather found the truth. Did he mention Project Prometheus in that little book of his? Mountain City Club. Tonight. Come and see what he died trying to expose.*

"The Mountain City Club?" Amelia frowned. "That's where half of Washington stays when they're in town."

"Yeah," Marshall said as she joined them at the table. "It's the perfect cover. We know that Hayes handled the research, and the

Caldwells provided the infrastructure, but someone pretty high up had to be pulling the strings."

"We go in hard," Jack said, still staring at his phone. "Full tactical support, CDC team standing by. After Hayes' surprise at the hospital…"

"I'll coordinate with Washington—" Marshall began, but Jack stopped her.

"No. Not yet," he said. "If this goes as high as we think, we need to know who we can trust first. We do this ourselves."

"What about Kate?" Amelia asked.

Jack thought for a moment, then said, "I'd better put her in the picture. Give me a minute."

He turned and walked away, already dialing his phone. He returned a moment later. "She wasn't happy, but when I asked what could possibly go wrong at the Mountain City Club, she agreed to go along with it. She'll be here as soon as she's finished filling in the chief."

"These funding traces," Amelia said. "Money flowing through the Caldwell foundations. Some of it was from legitimate mining operations, but most of it originated from classified government programs. Someone higher up was authorizing Hayes' work."

Jack studied his grandfather's notebook, looking for the Prometheus Project. His grandfather, Charles North, hadn't just been investigating corruption. It was beginning to look as if he'd uncovered a state-sponsored weapons program.

"He must have gotten too close," Marshall said quietly. "If he'd managed to connect Hayes' research to… I dunno, some official agency…"

"But he prepared for it," Amelia pointed out. "The hidden hospital systems, the override codes. He left us everything we'd needed."

Jack's phone buzzed again: *Eight o'clock. Mountain City Club. The man who signed your grandfather's death warrant wants to talk.*

"Another trap?" Amelia asked.

"I shouldn't wonder," Jack said. He sounded tired, and no wonder. He'd been at it for more than a week and with little in the way of rest.

"But we have to take the chance," he said. "It's the only way we're going to learn who's really behind all this."

He walked to the window and looked out across the city at the great bulk that was Lookout Mountain, and he wondered, *Is the answer really up there somewhere?*

He went back to the table, sat down, picked up his grandfather's notebook, and turned to the last pages. In Charlie's fine cursive handwriting, he'd written one last entry: *Follow the money!*

CHAPTER 24

Tuesday Evening

MOUNTAIN CITY CLUB
    Kate
    7:45pm

THE MOUNTAIN CITY CLUB was located on the west brow of Lookout Mountain. It was the epitome of exclusivity, its Georgian architecture illuminated by carefully placed lighting. It had been a bastion of political power for more than a century and a half.

Night had fallen, mist shrouded the crest of the mountain, when Jack parked his unmarked cruiser two blocks away and checked his equipment one last time.

"Surveillance confirms there are six government vehicles in the private lot," Amelia said through his earpiece. "Senator Porter's in there, along with two federal judges and what looks like military brass. Kate's team's in place and—"

"Jack," I said, interrupting her. "This is your show, but only because of your anonymous contact. You're to stay in contact and you don't do anything to escalate what could become an ugly political situation. Understand?"

"Yeah, Cap. I understand," Jack replied.

"We're here to back you," I continued. "If things go sideways, don't hesitate to holler. Check your wire and your watch. We can see what you see, and we'll have you on speaker." He was wearing a wire and a WiFi 1080P Security Camera Watch.

"Check," Jack said. "All is good. Now, can we do this, please?"

I heard Jack blow out a breath through closed lips, making a sound like a horse. I shook my head. He was obviously nervous, and there was nothing I could say to help him, other than we were in full communication and could hear everything that was going on. Now whether or not that helped, I don't know, but as I looked out through the car window at the club's façade I couldn't help but think it screamed old money. But the security—the cameras and the gate guard—all of that was modern and up to date.

"Jack," I said, quietly. "Remember, if this goes bad, you yell for help. We're not just dealing with local agencies anymore. These people can make whole agencies disappear."

"Got it," He replied. Then, after a brief pause, he said. "Okay, I'm going in."

"All teams are in position," Marshall confirmed quietly. "Kate, we have eyes on the place. Thermal. We count fifty-two heat signatures inside and four outside, and we have eyes on all exits. No one moves in or out without us seeing it."

I watched as Jack got out of the car and walked toward the front entrance.

"Detective Jack North," he said as he approached the doorman at the top of the steps. "I'm expected."

"You are indeed, sir. May I see your credentials?"

Jack handed the man his ID.

The man studied it intently. Looked at Jack several times,

then handed back the wallet and said, "Your phone, please, sir. You can collect it on the way out."

Jack handed him his phone.

"Thank you, sir. Now, if you'll follow me, Senator Porter is waiting for you."

Jack raised his left hand—the one with the watch—and placed it flat on his chest over his breast pocket, but only for a moment, to reveal a silver-haired man in an impeccably tailored suit approaching. "Detective North," he said, silkily, "Senator Porter sends his regrets. But Dr. Whitfield would like a word. In the private dining room."

"Whitfield?" Amelia sounded concerned. "Jack, that name's all over your grandfather's notes."

"This way, sir." The man gestured toward a hallway lined with dark wood panels.

Jack nodded and followed him, his hand now inside his jacket.

"Multiple heat signatures in the dining room," Marshall warned

The private dining room doors opened automatically at their approach to reveal a dozen men in expensive suits seated around a massive table.

"Good evening, Jack," the man at the head of the table said as he stood up, "I'm Dr. Marcus Whitfield, Director of Special Research Projects." He said pleasantly. "I knew your grandfather, Detective Charles North. Please, join us. We have much to discuss."

Jack stood for a moment as if he was hesitating, put his left hand to his chin and squeezed his lips together, giving us a wide-angle view of the table. I recognized two federal judges, Senator Porter, three congressmen and a general wearing Air Force insignia.

"Geez," I whispered. "This is unreal. Federal Judges Ambrose Jenkins and Reginald Smart. Air Force Major General Clement Hawkins, Congressman Hackman—"

"Sit down, Jack," I heard Whitfield say. "Your grandfather sat in that same chair nine years ago, shortly before his... unfortunate diagnosis. He'd made many of the same connections you have. Doctor Hayes' research. The Caldwell infrastructure. The military applications—"

"You ordered his death," Jack says quietly.

"Charlie was a good man," Whitfield said, dodging the question. "We offered him options. The same ones we're offering you now. His investigative skills made him... let's say... uniquely valuable. As are you."

"There's something happening in the basement," Marshall warned through his earpiece. "Multiple heat signatures."

"Your recent work has been impressive," Whitfield continued. "Dismantling Hayes' operation. Capturing the Caldwells. But surely you understand they were all just infrastructure. The real work, the necessary work, continues."

"The necessary work?" Jack said with his left hand resting on the table, the camera on Whitfield and Porter, who was sitting next to him on his left, keeping his voice level despite his rising anger. "You mean murdering people with engineered diseases? Testing bioweapons on American citizens?"

"Advancing human evolution," Senator Porter interjected. "Creating tools to protect our national interests."

"Your grandfather understood the science," Whitfield said, studying Jack over steepled fingers. "He saw the potential. Hayes' research, combined with our resources..." He gestured to the military and political figures seated around the table. "Imagine it. Perfect deniability. Being able to remove threats to national security without being scrutinized."

"Bullshit," Jack snapped. "My grandfather wouldn't have gone along with any such scheme, much less understand the science. He was a detective, not a scientist."

"True," Whitfield replied, smiling. "But your grandmother, she was different. She understood it only too well."

"My grandmother? What the hell are you talking about?"

But Whitfield merely smiled at him.

"Something's happening in the basement," Amelia warned him through his earpiece. "The readings are spiking in the ventilation system. I think they're trying something like Hayes did."

Jack bit his lip. He had no protection against a gas or biological attack, but then he realized neither did the people sitting around the table. *Can't be anything deadly,* he thought, then said, "You're all part of it." He looked at the two judges who were sitting together. "You buried evidence. You, Congressman Hackman... You and your two cronies approved the black budgets. And you, General Hawkins, you provided the test subjects. You're all either murders or conspirators to murder."

"We serve our country," the Air Force general said stiffly. "Sometimes that requires difficult decisions."

"Like murdering my grandfather?"

"Your grandfather chose his fate," Whitfield snapped. "He could have joined us, but instead he chose to expose a perfect program and thus became a perfect test case for Hayes' targeted delivery systems."

"You smug bastard," Jack snapped. "So now you're offering me the same choice?" Jack asked, buying time. "It's a case of join or die?"

"Join us," Whitfield said, "or become another data point in our research. Though I must admit, I'm curious to see how Hayes' latest refinements compare to what we used on your grandfather."

"Interesting choice of venue," Jack said, twisting around in his chair and sweeping the room with his watch, showing the positions of armed security personnel now visible at every exit. "The Mountain City Club. Where my grandfather made his last stand."

"Rather appropriate, don't you think?" Whitfield smiled. "Though we've made quite a few improvements since then. The ventilation system, for instance..."

"You mean the one delivering Hayes' newest compound right now?" Jack meets Whitfield's eyes. "The one my grandfather mapped eight years ago? Aren't you exposing yourselves?"

Whitfield's smile hardened, became humorless. "We're all inoculated against the agent, but not you, Detective." His expression changed. His eyes narrowed and then, as if he had a second thought, he said, "Yes, your grandfather's notes were quite thorough. But don't think for one minute—"

"That he found the original schematics?" Jack asked, interrupting him. "Hah, he found them all right." Jack smiled. "He was a lot smarter than you think."

"The system's shutting down!" Amelia shouted in his ear.

It was at that moment an alarm sounded. Whitfield jumped to his feet. "Seal all the exits!"

"Too late," Jack said calmly as federal agents breached the room's main doors.

"We got it all, gentlemen." He waved his watch for all to see. "We have every word you've uttered tonight, audio and video. It's all been broadcast to multiple agencies. Including the part about murdering Police Detective Charles North. There's no statute of limitation on capital murder. You're all going to prison for a very long time... Unless, of course, one of you wants to make a deal."

Jack stood by as I stepped into the room, followed by Marshall at the head of her tactical team, weapons trained on the security guards and dumbstruck power brokers. "Everyone stay where you are," I shouted. "You four, drop your weapons. Do it now."

I nodded to my officers and they stepped forward and quickly cuffed the guards.

Senator Porter's hand shook as he reached for his water glass. The rest of the cabal sat quietly. All of them in various states of shock.

Marshall handed Jack a piece of paper, smiled at him and said, "Would you like to do the honors, Detective?"

Jack looked at the paper and smiled. On it was a list of the names of everyone present.

He looked around the room, and then began, "Ironic, isn't it?" he said. "After all these years, and now, Doctor Marcus Whitman, Senator Robert Porter..." He continued to call out their names and then said, "You have the right to remain silent—"

"You have no idea what you're interfering with," Whitfield shouted, interrupting him. "The program is important to national security—"

"You mean your weapons program?" Marshall said. "The one that murdered American citizens as test subjects?"

She nodded to Jack for him to continue.

"You have the right to remain silent..." he began again, then ended with "do you all understand these rights?"

No one answered. They all sat staring stoically at him, most of them with their arms folded.

"Everything's documented," Jack said after a moment of silence. "Every project, every test subject, every death ordered by the people seated around this table. Including my grandfather's."

"That's impossible," Whitfield whispered. "The records were destroyed—"

"You still don't get it, do you?" Jack said. "Charlie North was a great detective. He made copies, and he left them where only another detective would think to look." He took his grandfather's notebook from his inside pocket and waved it in the air. "This has the locations. We have them. He knew what was happening to him. And he made sure someone would find them, and I did. You're done, Whitfield. You and your... co-conspirators are under arrest for first degree murder, conspiracy to murder, the illegal... human experimentation—"

"You stupid man," Whitfield snapped. "We're... patriots. We protected, are protecting... American interests—"

"By murdering American citizens?" Jack stepped around the table to stand behind Whitfield. "By using them as lab rats?"

"You just don't understand, do you? It was... beautiful," Whitfield's eyes took on a fevered gleam. "Each stage... precisely controlled." He looked around at Jack. "It's not over. Hayes monitored everything—"

Marshall stepped forward, handcuffs in hand, but Whitfield wasn't finished.

"Do you really think it ends here? With us?" He laughed. "You have absolutely no idea. Project Prometheus has branches everywhere, all over the world. We've spent decades—"

"And we have it all," Jack snapped, interrupting him. "Hayes was very thorough. She filed everything. Every record, every file, every connection, every little secret you thought was safely buried, even Operation Blackbriar during which, from 1987, you took test subjects from federal prisons, all of them listed as dead from natural causes. And then there's the Miami processing center, the Caldwell's transport network, and your system for shipping them through the caves and burying them there. We've found four bodies so far, but we know there are many more. The caves were the perfect cover, so you thought. But they're giving up their secrets. It's over, and thank God for it. You people are monsters."

"How many?" Marshall demanded. "How many people did you murder?"

No one answered.

"Hundreds?" she asked.

Again, no one answered.

"Thousands?" she asked.

It was Whitfield who spoke. "Each regrettable death was carefully studied and documented, proving our methods were, are, sound. As I said, we're not murderers as you put it; we're patriots saving America. The Prometheus Project..." he continued, "It was all legally done. Government contracts approved by Congress dating back to the Cold War, perfecting untraceable methods of elimination—"

"Where are they?" Marshall snapped. "The files."

Whitfield smiled. "So you don't have everything?" he said.

"There's a secure server here in the basement…" Porter said. He sounded tired. He looked at Whitfield and said, "It over, Marcus. I told you back then that North's death would one day bring us down, but you wouldn't have it. You and Hayes. All those people… My God, what have we done? And for what? This!" He waved his hand expansively, encompassing the entire room.

Jack retrieved his phone from the doorman and no sooner had he done so than it buzzed. He checked the message. *Well done, Detective. Your grandfather would be proud. But there's more. Are you ready to see how deep the rabbit hole really goes?*

Jack looked at Marshall and showed her the phone.

"Seriously?" she asked. "What are you going to do?"

"Reply, of course," he said. "What's the point of all this if we don't see it through to the end? But first we need to finish up here. What about the servers in the basement?"

Marshall nodded. "They're on it," she replied.

CHAPTER 25

Tuesday Evening

Mountain City Club
   Kate
   9:30pm

I stood by and watched as Marshall's people escorted the members of Project Prometheus out to the waiting vans. Meanwhile, Amelia and a team of forensic computer analysts were in the basement, tearing it apart.

Where was Samson while all this was going on, you might be wondering? Well, he was at my side as always, but on a short leash.

And Jack? I was worried about him. As far as I knew, he hadn't been to bed in three days.

"Hey," I said, touching him on the arm. "You okay?'

He gave me a tight smile, nodded, and said, "Yeah. I'm good."

"Well," I said. "Maybe you can get some sleep now."

He looked at me. "Yeah, but you need to see this." And he handed me his phone.

Well done, Detective," I read. *Your grandfather would be proud. But there's more. Are you ready to see how deep the rabbit hole really goes?*

I looked up at him and said, "What have you done about this?"

"Nothing yet," he replied. "But I think I need to answer it. We're obviously not at the bottom of this thing yet."

I was about to reply when Amelia said through our earpieces, "Jack, can you come down here? You need to see this."

He looked at me. I nodded. "We can talk about this later," I said as I handed the phone back to him. "Let's go see what she's found."

"Amelia?" Jack shouted as we stepped down into the basement, a vast concrete structure that seemed to go on forever.

"Back here," she said through our earpieces, "in the server room. Keep on coming. You'll see."

We found her at a computer monitor inside what easily could have passed for a concrete blockhouse studying something, while three computer techs were busy to her left at a bank of monitors.

"Hey, you made it," she said as we entered the room. "Come and take a look at these dates."

She watched over Jack's shoulder as Amelia flipped through the screens until she found the one she wanted. "There are projects going back to the sixties," she said. "Medical research, mostly... And these names" She paused, turned her head to look at him. "Jack, you... You..." She trailed off.

On her screen was what she later explained was a list of Project Prometheus board members and operatives through the years. She flipped the screen once and on the second page, near the top, I saw a familiar name: Lab Technician Martha North. *Geez,* I thought *Who the hell is that?*

He looked at it and nodded. "Yeah," he replied. "My grandmother. I knew she was a lab technician at one of the hospitals, but I never knew her. She died before I was born. What the hell?"

"What did she die of, d'you know?" Amelia asked.

Jack grimaced and shook his head. "No, as I said, it was before my time. She would have been about sixty, I guess."

"She was awful young," I said. "We need to look into it. Jack?"

"Easy enough," Jack replied. "I'll call my mother."

He looked at his watch. It was just after ten. "Bit late," he said, "but what the hell?"

He tapped the speed dial and waited.

"Mom, sorry to call so late, but it's urgent. I have a quick question. What did grandma Martha die of and when did she die...? Really...? You're sure...? Yeah, of course you are. Sorry. I'll talk to you tomorrow. Night." And he hung up.

"She died of pancreatic cancer June 7, 1987. She was sixty-one..." He was silent for a moment, then said, "So they killed her, too," he muttered.

Amelia put a hand on his arm and squeezed it, but she said nothing. I mean, what was there to say?

Jack's phone buzzed again. He opened the message, read it, stared at it, then said, "Who the hell is this?" And he handed the phone to me. "I tried to trace them." He said and shook his head. "No dice, burner phone."

You haven't replied to my last message, Detective, I read. *I quite understand. It's all a bit much, isn't it? By now, though, you should know why your grandfather never stopped digging, and how your grandmother died. I knew her quite well. Are you ready for more hard truths? Tomorrow, detective. I'll show you what your grandmother discovered.*

I looked at him. He shrugged. "Go home, Jack," I said. "You, too, Amelia. We'll talk about this tomorrow morning. My office. Nine o'clock sharp. In the meantime, get some rest, both of you."

"Wait," Amelia said. "Jack. This is a list of personnel files from the '80s... your grandmother wasn't just a victim. She worked on the original research program at the Oakwood Medical Center."

Jack stared at her, obviously trying to process this new revelation, but before he could speak, Agent Marshall joined us and handed me a worn file folder. "We found this in Whitfield's private safe," she said. "It's labeled, Martha North, so I figured you'd better see it."

I opened it, glanced at the first page, closed it again and handed it to Jack.

He took it from me, looked at me, then opened it. Inside, I knew, were several official documents, the margins filled with comments in what obviously was a woman's cursive handwriting, and on the front page, a bio sheet, a photo of a woman in a lab coat. It was Martha North, I had no doubt. She was standing before the Oakwood Medical Center sign. On the back of the bio, written in her hand, were the words, 'The truth is in Lab 7.'

CHAPTER 26

Wednesday Morning

OAKWOOD MEDICAL CENTER

Kate

10am

AFTER THAT, I insisted that we all go home and get some rest. At the time, I was convinced that we'd broken the back of this thing and that all that was left was the mopping up. Boy, was I ever wrong.

Samson and I arrived at my office early the following morning, Wednesday, as always, at a little after eight. I settled him down in his bed under the window, made a pot of coffee and watched it brew.

Corbin arrived next at precisely eight-thirty, followed by Hawk, Ramirez and Cooper, in that order.

I took their reports and sent them on their way to their respective projects, retaining only my partner, Corbin.

I'd been keeping him up to date with Jack's investigations as the days passed, but now I figured that as I was now as deeply involved as was Jack, it made sense to get him involved too, so I spent the next twenty minutes bringing him up to speed.

Amelia arrived first at a little before nine. Jack arrived ten minutes later looking like... I'm going to say it: he looked like shit.

"Geez, just look at you," I said.

"Yeah, well," he said. "I didn't sleep hardly any, did I? What d'you expect?"

"There's coffee in the pot," I said. "Pour yourself a cup and sit down."

"I'd rather get—"

"I don't care what you'd rather get," I said. "We're waiting for Sarah Marshall. Now do as I say and sit down."

Reluctantly, he did as he was told. He poured himself some coffee and dropped into the seat at the round table next to Corbin, who grinned at him. "Rough week, I hear."

"You could say that," Jack answered, truculently. "Look, you said we'd talk about the text... the texts. So what's the plan, Captain?"

Jack rarely called me captain, usually only when he was pissed off, which he obviously was.

"Ah, the texts..." I said. "Somebody out there knows one hell of a lot and is feeding it to us... to you, in drips and drabs. You say you don't know who it could be and if, as you say, that person is using a burner phone we may never know—"

There was, at that moment, a knock on the door. It opened, and Sarah Marshall stuck her head in and said, "I'm not too late, I hope."

"Nope," I replied. "Come on in. You want some coffee?"

"Nah," she replied. "I've had plenty." And she sat down at the table next to Amelia.

"You have the warrant?" I asked.

She nodded. "Last night. Knocked up Judge Allan. He wasn't pleased, but he signed it." She grinned at me.

"Good. We were discussing the texts someone's been sending to Jack," I said. "Any thoughts?"

She pursed her lips and shook her head. "You tried tracing them?"

"Puh! Yeah," Jack said, dryly. "They're using a burner."

"Any other news?" I asked.

"Nothing you don't already know. I have agents on their way to the Oakwood Medical Center. They should be arriving anytime now. I gave instructions to secure the place and wait for us."

"Well then," I said, "if there's nothing else…" I looked around. Nobody spoke. "Then let's go. Come on, Sammy."

I KNEW where the Oakwood Medical Center on Jersey Pike was. I also knew that, like the Old County Hospital, it had been closed for years. Unlike the County Hospital, though, the abandoned medical center looked almost cheery by comparison. A low, two-story, white building, it stretched for almost a block in each direction with a long parking area, four lots deep, running the entire front of the building. It was one of those nondescript structures one drives by but rarely notices.

I had Corbin with me—Samson in the back seat, his nose on the console between us, as we pulled into the lot, followed by Jack and Amelia, then Agent Marshall.

As Marshall had said, her agents were already there and had the place secured.

"It's been vacant since '89," Marshall said as we joined her at the hood of her car. She was checking blueprints of the building on her iPad. "Or supposedly vacant, but there are lights on inside." She nodded at the front entrance. She was right. There was indeed a light on in the foyer.

"Let's do this," Jack muttered as he went around to the trunk of his car, opened it and took out a large pair of bolt cutters.

He quickly cut the tang of the padlock and grabbed the handle. The door was locked.

"Damn it," he muttered and looked at Amelia.

She smiled at him. "Not one of your skills, I take it?"

"I could bust it in," he replied, "but why risk hurting myself when you're so… skillful?"

She laughed. She had the door open in less than thirty seconds; no damage done.

"Right," Jack said. "Lab 7. Where is it?"

"Wait," I said, sharply. "Let's not rush into this. We need to comms up and stay in touch. Sarah, we need to clear the building before we go rushing it. You have thermal imaging?"

She nodded. "Give me a minute." And she went to her car, said something over the radio, listened for several minutes, then returned and said, "The drone's up. It looks like we're not alone. Thermal imaging shows multiple heat signatures on the north-west side of the building."

"According to the blueprints," Marshall said, "the labs were on the first floor, at the south end of the building. Lab 7 is at the southeast corner."

We made our way along the corridor, passing empty offices, papers still scattered on the desks and the floors, as if the evacuation had happened only yesterday instead of decades ago.

"Movement to the northwest," Marshall warned through comms. "Looks like they're heading this way."

I eased my Glock 17 out of its holster and watched as Jack did the same. And we proceeded south along the corridor, Samson trotting at my heels.

The corridor ended at a pair of heavy double doors marked "Laboratory 7 - Restricted Access." I peered through wire-reinforced windows and could see that the lights were on and there was movement within.

To step into Lab 7 was to step back in time. A relic from the 1960s and 70s: glass-fronted cabinets filled with neatly labeled specimen jars and research equipment lined the walls. On the central workspace: microscopes and testing apparatus that probably belonged in a museum. Metal cabinets filled with folders yellowed with age.

Jack and I, with Amelia close behind, stepped inside, weapons drawn.

"There's no need for weapons," the figure at the lab bench said without turning.

An elderly woman of Asian extraction, slim, tall, her silver hair pulled back in a severe bun, wore a faded ID badge on her lab coat that proclaimed her to be Dr. Margaret Lu.

"Doctor Lu," Amelia whispered. "She was Martha North's boss."

Lu turned from the ancient centrifuge she's been adjusting. "That's true, my dear," she said. "Welcome to where it all began. Martha did her best work here. Before she developed a conscience. Detective North," she continued, smiling at him as he holstered his Glock. "I've heard so much about you." She put a hand on the bench. "Your grandmother worked at this bench," she said, running her fingertips over the scarred surface. "Martha kept meticulous notes. She recorded everything. Test subjects coming in healthy, leaving sick. Military officers meeting with Dr. Hayes after hours. She was so smart. She pieced it all together, bit by bit. When she died, I gathered it up and hid it. I gave your grandfather access to it when he came to me. It's what got him killed. Oh, and yes, I knew you were coming, Detective. Someone—I don't know who—texted me. Anyway... It's no use to me. I'll be seventy-nine this year and I'm not feeling well. It seems they may have gotten to me, too. So, I brought it here for you."

"You were the person sending me the texts, right?" Jack asked.

"Texts?" She frowned. "I'm sorry, I don't know what you're talking about. I sent no texts."

"Huh!" Jack said, also frowning. "Then who... Never mind. Please continue."

Lu nodded, pulled open a drawer and took out a well-worn three-inch ring binder, placed it on the bench and opened it. Even from where I was, several paces from the bench, I could see its pages were filled with Martha's neat script.

"Daily observations," Lu continued almost dreamily. "Which doctors handled which patients. The 'special protocols' they claimed were experimental treatments. Martha saw how the symptoms matched specific test groups."

Lu paused for a moment, then continued. "She knew immediately, of course. She'd documented those exact symptoms for years." Lu turned the pages slowly, reflectively. "The progressive deterioration, the specific markers; she'd seen it all before. It was then that she began gathering proof, using her position as a trusted lab tech to access records no one thought she'd understand."

"They underestimated her, then?" Amelia asked.

"Fatally." Lu stepped over to the old steel file cabinet. "She left most of it here." She pulled open a drawer and shut it again; it made a hollow sound. "It's all gone now, but the evidence that could shut down Project Prometheus is in that binder. Evidence your grandfather used when he got too close to the truth. He never got over her death, you know. She cataloged everything," Lu said as she moved to a cabinet with closed doors and a patted the top. "Patient records showing identical symptoms in people who'd threatened the program. Chemical formulas she copied in secret. Delivery methods disguised as routine treatments. Everything. All gone now. Hayes saw to that."

She opened the cabinet door and lifted out a small wooden

box. "This was Martha's," she said as she set it on the bench and opened it.

Jack and I stepped forward together. The box was filled with photocopies of classified military documents describing targeted elimination, a long list of victims with matching symptoms, notes she'd written documenting everything and where to find it, even a letter she'd written but never mailed in case she was next.

"Like your grandfather, she knew too much," Lu continued. "And then she complained she wasn't feeling well. Dr. Hayes suggested she undergo some 'precautionary tests.' Martha recognized the pattern - she'd seen it too many times before…"

The room was quiet. Lu stared down at the contents of the box, touched the edge with a finger. "Too bad," she whispered.

"Go on," Jack said.

She looked at him. "There's little more I can tell you," she said. "Except for this." She took a slim folder, sealed in plastic, from the cabinet. "This is what they really feared: proof their perfect weapon had a flaw. Something only a technician who'd watched it being developed would notice. This file contains Martha's observations of test subjects who showed unexpected immunity. Notes about chemical variations that produced resistance. Details that could unravel decades of weapons development. As I said, I gave your grandfather access to all this," she waved her hand over the box and the file, "and he used it to build his case. Unfortunately, they got to him before he could bring them down. Now it's your turn." She handed Jack the folder. "Finish what your grandparents died trying to expose."

"Multiple heat signatures at the far end of the corridor," Marshall warned through their earpieces.

"They're coming," Amelia said. "We need to get out of here."

I could tell Samson knew something was happening. He was facing the door, ridged, hackles raised, his ears flattened, on point.

I could hear voices, shouting, running footsteps, approaching fast. Samson did a little dance, straining at his leash.

"The door's locked," Amelia snapped, "but it won't hold them for long. Is there another way out?"

"Wait. I want you to take this, too," Lu said, taking a small vial from her lab coat pocket and handing it to Jack. "This is what Martha was working on when they came for her. Get it to someone who can analyze it properly."

"We need to get out of here." Amelia was close to panic.

"The emergency exit," Lu said. "It opens into the southwest parking area. Follow me."

Jack and I grabbed the files and the box and we followed her through a door at the end of the lab into another, smaller room, where on the far wall was a steel door with a panic bar.

I hit the bar with my right hand. The door swung open and we ran out into the weak winter sunshine.

I stopped and turned to see Lu pulling the door shut.

"You need to come with us," I shouted. "They'll know you helped us."

She paused, smiled at me and said, "No. I can buy you some time... I've lived with this guilt for forty years. Maybe I'll get what I deserve. Go!" And the door slammed shut.

"Multiple heat signatures entering Lab 7," Marshall snapped through the comms. "More at the perimeter. My team's moving in."

We ran around the south end of the building to the front where our vehicles were parked along with a dozen emergency vehicles, marked and unmarked, their lights flashing.

"Made it," Marshall said as we made it to the cars.

"What about Lu?" Amelia asked, breathlessly.

"She knew what she was doing," Jack said, staring back at the building. "I wonder if she's still alive."

I was wondering the same thing, but we never found out. Dr. Lu disappeared that day and was never seen again.

IT WAS a little after noon when we arrived back at the command center, having left a combined task force of twenty-two officers and agents to mop up the mess at the Oakwood Medical Center and to try to rescue Dr. Lu. But, as I already mentioned, that didn't happen. Nor were they able to capture any of the intruders. By the time our people reached Lab 7, they were all long gone, Dr. Lu with them, so it seemed. Me? I like to think the wily old bird had a little something left up her sleeve and had made it out of there unscathed. Wishful thinking? Perhaps, but she'd been savvy enough to make it safely through the almost forty years since Martha North died, so who knows? One can hope, right?

We spread Martha's legacy across the conference table. It was amazing to see how her detailed logs showed how Project Prometheus had evolved from medical research to weaponized formulas, documented by a mere lab tech who saw, and understood, everything.

"Unbelievable," Marshall said. "Forty years worth of evidence, all collected by someone they thought was just a nobody following orders."

"I'm sure she knew the risks," Amelia said.

It was around five that afternoon when my phone rang. It was the FBI lab with an update on the vial Lu gave to Jack. "The compound contains encoded genetic markers linked to specific DNA sequences," the lab tech said. It was an antidote, Martha North's own formula, her protection against whatever it was they'd created. *I wonder why she didn't use it.* I thought, frowning. *It could have saved her life. Maybe she did use it. Maybe it didn't work.*

I heaved a sigh, reached down, and ruffled the fur at the back of Sammy's ears.

"It looks like we have enough to take down their entire network. Martha's evidence, along with what we've already found, is pretty damning: It connects it all together—the research, the murders, the government contracts. All hell's going to break loose when this hits the fan." Then I had a horrible thought, *If it ever does hit the fan.*

"She left a letter," I said. "It's addressed to you, Jack." I handed him the envelope I found from the evidence box. It had his name on it, but I've seen enough of her handwriting to know it wasn't written by Martha. Lu, perhaps?

He opened it, read it, and then, without a word, handed it to me.

The letter itself *was* in Martha's handwriting.

To whomever finds this,

I hope you are family, and I hope you understand why we have to fight them. They thought I was just a lab tech, too simple to comprehend their work. That blindness was their weakness. While they watched the doctors and researchers, they never noticed me documenting everything. I know my notes and research are the best chance for justice for all their victims, and there are a lot of them. But if you're reading this, then I have failed. You must not fail. You are their only hope. Be careful. Be thorough. And above all, be smarter than they think you are.

With love,

Martha.

I handed it back to Jack and watched as he carefully refolded it and slipped it back into its envelope.

"This is mine," he said, locking eyes with me as he slipped it into the inside pocket of his jacket. "We'll finish it. For both of them."

I nodded. What else could I do?

It was, by then, getting late, and we were all tired and ready to call it a day when Jack's phone buzzed.

He checked the screen, looked at me, and nodded, and handed me the phone.

Your grandparents built the case, Detective. Now it's time for you to close it. Tomorrow. 9pm. The River City Club. The board wants to discuss surrender terms.

CHAPTER 27

Thursday

THE RIVER CITY CLUB
    Kate
    8pm

HERE WE ARE AGAIN, I thought as Jack and I exited my unmarked cruiser. I'd left Samson at home curled up in his bed, and we were now parked outside the River City Club along with three blue and white police cruisers and four black Chevy Suburbans, Agent Sarah Marshall and her team's transportation.

It was another of those wild nights in late November when the clouds were hanging low over the mountaintop and hurling rain down upon us in bucketfuls. Yup, it was one hell of a night to be doing what we were about to do, and I feared it boded ill for us. Still, we'd been summoned by Jack's unknown texting bene-factor so we had no choice. After all, whoever it was that was texting Jack had been right… up until then.

Dark as the night was, the Georgian hulk looked even darker.

Its doric columns and brick facade softly illuminated in the pouring rain every once in a while by a flash of lightning. We might as well have been acting out one of those old Hammer Horror movies.

Inside, the polished oak paneling and crystal chandeliers glistened in the artificial light. *What generations of deals that have shaped history have they witnessed?* I wondered. *What kind of deal will they witness tonight? For deal it will be. These sons o' bitches always seem to be able to cut a deal, don't they?*

Yes, I was... upset. We were about to take down some of the highest level operators in Washington and at the Pentagon, but I figured they were probably going to get away with it, as they always did.

"Security teams are in position," Marshall's voice came over the comms. "All exits are covered. We confirm ten Project Prometheus board members are present in the conference room. And it appears they've cleared out the regular staff. Just the board members and their security detail remain."

I watched as Jack adjusted his tie. I knew he had his grandfather's notebook and Martha's binder and file in a briefcase at his side.

The doorman—a private security officer—the same one from two nights ago, gave us a respectful nod as we stepped past him into the grand foyer.

"If you'll follow me," he said, and led the way to the conference room.

As we stepped inside, I had to smile to myself. They were seated around a long and vast expanse of mahogany that was the conference table. Ten figures seated around it like a corporate last supper. Ten expensive suits, military ribbons, federal credentials displayed with casual arrogance. These men and women were the true face of Project Prometheus.

Seated at the head of the table, I recognized General Andrew Mitchell, Chairman of the Joint Chiefs of Staff and the program's military commander. He was in full uniform. The four stars on his shoulders glittering in the light of the chandeliers, his chest heavy with decorations, his manner suggesting he was someone who was used to being obeyed.

To his right was the secretary of defense. To his left, the secretary of the air force and the surgeon general of the United States. And there were people I'd never seen or heard of, but by their attire they were beyond important. I learned later that some of them were the scientists who developed the weapons. All of them watching us, especially Jack, with predatory focus.

"Detective North," Mitchell stood up, his posture parade-ground perfect. "Thank you for coming. We're prepared to offer terms."

"Terms?" Jack asked, sarcastically. He, that is we, remained standing by the door, noting the positions of armed security personnel. "Are you kidding? You're all murderers."

"We understand recent events have... shifted the balance of power." Mitchell was obviously choosing his words carefully. "Dr. Lu's last act at Oakwood demonstrated certain vulnerabilities in our position. We're prepared to discuss a... mutually beneficial resolute—"

The soft click of heels on the polished wood floor interrupted his obviously well-prepared and practiced speech.

The heels were those of Margaret Wheeler, Mitchell's secretary. She entered the room through a side door and moved quickly to the general's side with the quiet efficiency that had made her virtually invisible to the powerful men she served.

"The usual files, General?" Her voice carried subtle authority as she places the folder before Mitchell. Her silver hair perfectly coifed, pearls gleaming, her designer suit evidence of her senior administrative status... and salary.

"That will be all, thank you, Margaret. You may go now," Mitchell said without even glancing at her.

"Actually, General," she said as she straightened the papers. "I believe I'll stay." She looked straight at Jack and then continued, "You see, Detective North... those texts and messages you've been receiving... they were from me." And she smiled at him.

The room went still, quiet.

"Messages, texts?" Mitchell's voice sounded deadly. "What... in God's name d'you mean?"

"Since 1974, I've documented everything," she said calmly, still arranging the papers. "Martha North showed me how. You see, it's the quiet ones, the invisible ones. We see everything, don't we, Detective? Your grandmother taught me that."

"You knew her?" Jack asked, his brow furrowed.

"We started work the same week. She in the lab, me in the office." Margaret's voice never wavered. "I helped her access files and... I watched them kill her."

At that, several of the Project Prometheus board members shifted uneasily in their chairs. Mitchell's face darkened as he stared at his diminutive but trusted secretary of more than twenty-five years.

"Every meeting," Margaret continued, adjusting her pearls. "Every decision. Every murder ordered from this very room. All documented, all secured. Just waiting for someone smart enough to follow the trail." She looked at Jack. "Like your grandmother, I learned how to hide in plain sight."

"Margaret," Mitchell snapped. "Think very carefully about what you're doing."

"Oh, I have, General," she replied. "For twenty-five years I have." She moved away from his chair. "Did you never wonder how Charles North got those files? How he knew exactly where to look?" She smiled. "You had Martha murdered, didn't you? But you never noticed me, did you? You people never do. You never notice your secretaries making copies, do you, General? I hope you and your cronies rot in jail for what you did."

"Security," Mitchell barked, but Margaret shook her head.

"I'm afraid they're rather busy at the moment," she said. "Oh and by the way, some interesting documents just landed on certain desks in Washington. Amazing what a senior administrator's clearance can do, isn't it?"

We watched her as she crossed to our side of the table. Every eye in the room followed her as she stepped confidently around behind Mitchell.

Mitchell leaped to his feet, his face red with anger, his chair scraping the floor. "You just signed your death warrant, Margaret."

"Have I?" She opened her tablet. "Interesting choice of words, General,considering how many of those you've signed in this very room." Her fingers danced over the screen. "There," she said, "That's the lot. I just sent the rest of the files to the Secretary of Homeland Security. Every order, every signature, every project authorization. That should do it, I think," she looked around the table, "for the lot of you."

"Our security teams—" one of the federal judges began but was interrupted by the general..

"You were my secretary," Mitchell's voice quavered, filled with disbelief.

"I was your archivist," she corrected him. "I recorded your crimes. Watching, waiting, building the case. You rarely even acknowledged my presence. But that's how it is with the rich and powerful. You take everything for granted. You never notice the quiet ones, do you? That was your weakness."

"General Andrew Mitchell," Marshall stepped forward. "You and your board members are under arrest for conspiracy, murder, and illegal weapons development, and God only knows what else."

"You have no authority—" Mitchell began.

"Actually," Margaret said, interrupting him, "The United States Attorney General personally signed the arrest warrants an hour ago. Along with authorization for a full investigation into Project Prometheus. Amazing how quickly people act when faced with decades of corruption and the documented evidence."

Mitchell stared at his secretary. "All this time..."

"You're an arrogant man, Andrew," she said. "You should have paid more attention to what was going on around you."

She turned to look at Jack. "Your grandmother would be proud of you, Detective. Both of them would be."

Jack smiled at her and nodded slightly and we watched as Marshall's federal agents cuffed Mitchell and his board members; decades of power stripped away in a moment.

Jack and I joined Margaret at the window, watching the rain and the occasional flash of lightning over the Lookout Valley. The storm was abating. *Another omen?* I wondered.

"I kept their photos," she said quietly, without turning her head. "Martha at her lab bench, your grandfather at his desk. I kept them as reminders of why I had to stay. I knew that one day..."

Seven hours later, in the FBI command center, I stood at the window and watched the dawn break, casting beams of golden sunlight through the dissipating clouds onto Lookout Mountain. It was going to be a beautiful day.

Behind me, Jack, Amelia, Sarah Marshall and her team had begun to sift through the mountain of evidence. Margaret Wheeler, pale faced, was seated at the far end of the room watching, and I couldn't help but wonder what she was thinking. twenty-five years of... 'devoted' service gone in an instant. It must have been devastating for her.

"The Attorney General's office is moving fast," Marshall said as she joined me at the window. "With Margaret's records and Jack's grandparents' evidence, we've got them cold."

I turned away from the window and looked around the busy room.

"It's hard to believe," I said, "that all this started in a cave with the discovery of a skeletal hand." I shook my head. My job has its up moments, and down. This was one of the ups, but somehow, I didn't feel quite as elated as I should. Jack had solved the mystery of Forrest's Cave and the deaths of his grandparents, and we'd stopped a five-decade long criminal enterprise that had reached into the highest levels of government, but now, standing in that room, it all seemed a little… anticlimactic.

Jack paused what he was doing and slowly picked up a photograph, and then another, and stared at them for a moment, then he looked up at me, came around the table and showed them to us.

"My grandparents," he said.

One was of Martha in a lab coat, standing at her bench smiling at the camera. The other was of Charlie North standing at a whiteboard, his suit jacket drawn back, hands in his pants pockets, showing his badge on his belt and the grip of his service revolver in its holster under his left arm. He, too, was smiling at the camera. Two people who'd died horribly fighting corruption, brought together in their grandson's investigation. *Kind of ironic*, I thought.

Jack looked at the photos thoughtfully, then replaced them in evidence.

"I wonder if there are more caves to explore?" he muttered.

EPILOGUE

One Month Later

JACK

THE NEW HEADSTONE gleamed in the morning sunlight. Charles and Martha North, finally resting side by side with the epitaph, 'They Never Gave Up," etched in granite.

Jack, flowers in hand, stood with Amelia in the Chattanooga National Cemetery, his head bowed, eyes closed. Amelia slipped her hand into his and squeezed it. Jack placed the flowers in front of the headstone, his other hand still holding Amelia's, then he stood for a moment, turned his head to look at her, smiled, then whispered, "Thank you for everything. Let's go get something to eat."

"The Attorney General's office called Marshall," she said as they walked slowly back to his car. "It seems Mitchell and the entire board have accepted plea deals in exchange for their silence."

"Of course they did," Jack said. "The bastards'll get away with it, just as people like them always do. No doubt they'll get a slap on the wrist and a hefty fine, and that will be it."

"They're naming the new ethics oversight committee after your grandparents," Amelia said, swinging their hands as they walked. "They're calling it the North Commission. Margaret's going to be a special advisor."

"If I know her, she probably has more files," Jack said with a smile.

They arrived at the passenger side of the car a few moments later and, before he opened the door for her, he turned to face her, took her other hand in his and, as she turned to face him, he saw in her eyes the same intensity that first caught his attention in Forrest's Cave.

"You know," she said as he was about to speak, "there are other cave systems that need exploring. Other secrets waiting to be uncovered. What do you think?" she asked, though from her smile he could tell she already knew the answer.

He pulled her closer. "Partners?" he asked.

"Partners," she agreed, reaching up to kiss him. "In everything."

THANK YOU FOR READING *THE MYSTERY OF FORREST'S CAVE*: BOOK 21 OF THE LT. KATE GAZZARA SERIES. WE HOPE YOU ENJOYED THESE STORIES AND WILL CONTINUE READING MORE BOOKS FROM BLAIR HOWARD. THE NEXT BOOK IN THIS SERIES IS BOOK 22: *BAD MEMORIES*

.

WAYS TO GET NOTIFIED OF NEW RELEASES:

FOLLOW ON AMAZON, BOOKBUB, AND JOIN THE AUTHORS EMAIL LIST.

SIGN UP For Announcements & great deals from the
author on his website!
All Paperbacks are signed and priced at **$9.99!**
Get Exclusive Deals (As Part Of "The Family")
Visit www.BlairHowardBooks.com

Don't forget to confirm your email and whitelist (save as
contact)BlairHoward@blairhowardbooks.com to your email
system.

FROM THE AUTHOR

THIS IS WHAT I KNOW, OR THINK I KNOW, ABOUT THE CAVES ON LOOKOUT MOUNTAIN TENNESSEE AND GEORGIA.

THE CAVES BENEATH LOOKOUT MOUNTAIN are a constant source of fascination, and while The Mystery of Forrest's Cave is a work of fiction, as is Forrest's Cave itself, the vast network of caves that inspired it is very real.

With over 200 documented caves, Lookout Mountain contains one of the most extensive cave systems in the United States. The limestone bedrock, formed millions of years ago from ancient seabeds, has been slowly dissolved by slightly acidic rainwater, creating a labyrinth of passages.

Ruby Falls, the mountain's most famous cave formation, represents just one small part of this vast underground realm. Many of these caves interconnect in ways the experts are still mapping. Local cavers regularly discover new passages linking what once were thought to be separate systems.

Local speleologists share tales of Civil War artifacts discovered in unnamed caves, Native American pictographs in chambers that hadn't seen light for centuries, and mapping passages that seemed to go on endlessly.

Modern mapping techniques suggest the existence of extensive unexplored passages, hinting at a hidden world that could dwarf what we currently know. It was this sense of mystery—the knowledge that we're surrounded by unexplored wonders—that inspired much of this story's atmosphere.

A final note of caution: while the caves in this novel are fictional, the dangers of amateur cave exploration are real. The mountain's caves demand respect, proper equipment, and experienced guidance. Anyone interested in exploring should contact the Southeastern Cave Conservancy or local authorized tour operators.

Long before European settlers arrived, the Cherokee called Lookout Mountain Enchanted Mountain. Their legends spoke of passages that ran through its heart, of underground rivers and hidden chambers. Some of these tales would later prove remarkably accurate.

The first documented cave exploration occurred in 1834 when an entrance high on the western slope was discovered. The descriptions of vast chambers and underground waterfalls sparked interest among early settlers.

During the Civil War, both Union and Confederate forces used the caves extensively.

The mining era brought systematic exploration. Between 1880 and 1920, mining companies mapped hundreds of passages while extracting gold, copper, quicksilver, coal, limestone, saltpeter, and other minerals. Many of their tunnels intersected with natural cave formations, creating the complex network that exists today.

The discovery of Ruby Falls in 1928 demonstrates how the mountain could still hold surprises. The 145-foot underground waterfall became one of the area's most famous attractions, yet it represents only a fraction of the cave system's extent.

Modern exploration continues to reveal new passages. In 2019, cavers discovered a previously unknown chamber containing prehistoric artifacts. Geological surveys suggest that less than half of the mountain's cave system has been fully explored.

Key Facts about Lookout Mountain's Caves:

- Over 200 documented caves
- Over 50 miles of mapped passages
- Depths ranging from near surface to over 1,000 feet
- Multiple underground streams and rivers
- Several rare species of cave-dwelling creatures
- Geological features dating back millions of years

The caves remain both a natural wonder and a subject of ongoing scientific research and, while this novel takes creative liberties with certain aspects, the real caves of Lookout Mountain continue to guard their own mysteries.

Blair Howard 2025

Short Stories and Novellas

Buried Secrets(Harry Starke)

The Painted Lady(Kate Gazzara)

Stand Alone

Hunter's Moon(Kate & Harry)

Series

The Harry Starke Genesis Series

9 Books in Series as of 2025

The Harry Starke Series

26 Books in Series as of October 2025

The Lt. Kate Gazzara Murder Files

22 Books in Series as of October 2025

Randall And Carver Mysteries

4 Books in Series as of October 2025

The Peacemaker Series

3 Books in Series as of October 2025

The O'Sullivan Chronicles: Civil War Series

5 Books in Series as of October 2025

Science Fiction From Blair C. Howard

The Sovereign Star Series

7 Books in Series as of October 2025

also available in German

The Predecessors Series

The Last Station-Book One

The Infinity War-Book Two

ABOUT THE AUTHOR

Blair Howard is the international best-selling author of more than seventy novels that span the worlds of gritty detective fiction, espionage thrillers, sweeping historicals, and hard-science military space opera. A Royal Air Force veteran and former journalist, he draws upon a rich background of service and storytelling to breathe life into unforgettable characters such as ex-cop turned private eye Harry Starke, and the fiercely determined homicide detective Lt. Kate Gazzara, who breaks her own trail as the head of a serious-crimes unit.

Under his sci-fi pen name Blair C. Howard, he expands his reach into the cosmos with the Sovereign Stars saga—an epic journey born from his lifelong love of the heavens, and the Predecessors hard science fiction trilogy. Whether unraveling a brutal crime scene or commanding starships in interstellar conflict, his stories are propelled by relentless pacing, vivid realism, and a watchful eye for justice.

www.BlairHowardBooks.com